Catcher

The 4 Seats
Book 4

Cassandra Doon

Independently published by Cassandra Doon

Edited by TJ's Editing Services

First Published November 2024

Edition 2 2026

Cover design by ANK Book Designs

Interior design by Vellum

Author Website: Cassandradoon.com

Author's Note

Dear Reader,

Before you begin this journey with Catcher and Posey, I want to take a moment to speak with you about the nature of this book and the subject matter it explores. This story is a return to the dark, intense, and gritty world you experienced in the earlier books of this series.

On the Subject of Underground Fight Clubs

In this book, we delve into the brutal world of underground fight clubs. These are places where the rules of society don't apply, and men often fight until the death. Some of these fighters are forced into this life, while others do it for the money or because they have a certain kind of madness that only the cage can satisfy.

I want to be honest with you: I chose to focus primarily on Catcher's side of this world. I didn't feel I had enough research on the intricate, often horrific details of how these clubs are run or the full extent of the trauma inflicted on every participant to write about it with the depth it truly requires. Because of this, I have kept the focus on Catcher's experience and his perspective, rather than trying to provide an exhaustive look at the industry itself.

On the Subject of Human Trafficking and Miscarriage

Like the previous book in this series, we continue to touch on the global crisis of human sex trafficking. It is a horrific violation of human rights that I refuse to romanticize. The darkness and exploitation are presented as the grave injustices they are, while the romance is reserved for the healing and connection between our main characters.

This story also explores the deeply personal and painful experience of miscarriage. This is a subject that affects many, and I have tried to handle it with the gravity and care it deserves. It is a moment of profound loss and change for both Catcher and Posey, and it plays a significant role in their journey together.

My Commitment to You

My commitment as a writer is to tell stories that matter, even when they are difficult. I want to handle sensitive subjects with care while creating characters you will root for and celebrate. While this journey is dark and often violent, I promise you that every book in this series ends with a Happily Ever After (HEA). Each story stands alone, and each couple finds their way to a satisfying conclusion.

Thank you for taking this journey with me. Thank you for caring about these characters and for your continued support.

With gratitude and respect,
Cassandra XXX

For the ones who spot red flags from across the room and, instead of legging it, saunter straight toward them—because we both know that's where the fun (and the tears) live.

And for you, Heathcliff—I see you, brooding in the corner like a walking tree-sized warning sign. I clock the flag, and I'm still happy to follow you into the dark.

Welcome Back, Dark Mafia Romance Readers.

Before you dive into the world of Catcher and Posey, here is a list of what is inside this book. Please don't read if anything here bothers you. Your mental health and comfort are paramount.

- •Extreme Violence & Gore
- •Torture & Interrogation
- •Non-Consensual Death
- •Trafficking & Sexual Exploitation
- •Snuff Themes
- •Miscarriage & Loss
- •Kidnapping & Captivity
- •Strong Language
- •Possessive/Controlling Behaviour

To everyone who reads this, like a shipping list:
Welcome back.

Chapter 1

Catcher

I stand at the back of the room, a ghost in the corner, my arms crossed over my chest; a posture that's become as much a part of me as my own skin. The air is thick with the metallic scent of fear, cheap perfume and a cocktail that clings to the back of my throat; a weight that I've learned to ignore but can never quite shake that settles somewhere deep in my chest. It's a familiar smell, one that used to mean nothing more than another Tuesday night, just another job with another set of faces that would blur together by the end of the week. Now, it just tastes like ash on my tongue, bitter and choking, a reminder of something I'm trying very hard not to feel. We're in an old warehouse that Gabe's father uses for this kind of sordid business. It's a cavernous space that sprawls across a large area and has seen more misery than a battlefield and more suffering than a prison.

My eyes are fixed on Gabe. He stands in the centre of the room, a stark figure against the grimy beige, water-stained exposed brick walls that are peeling in places and seem to weep with the misery of this place. There's a smell underneath the sickly-sweet perfume that the women wear, it's a mixture of fear, mould, and the stench of human suffering that's seeped into more than just the very foundations of this building. He's the heir to the Italian throne of Melbourne's underworld, the golden boy who was always destined for greatness, who is also meant to be my boss, but he's always just been Gabe to me. The kid I grew up with, the one whose back I've always had and the one I'll follow into hell itself without question. His father, the real king, the man who built an empire on blood and broken bones, is set to hand over the crown in two weeks. Two weeks. And this is how Gabe is spending his final days as a prince: cataloguing human misery, documenting the destruction of lives, playing the part of a monster so convincingly that sometimes I wonder if he's still in there at all.

He holds a Polaroid camera in his hands, a relic from another time that belongs in a museum or a dusty attic, but for this it serves its purpose perfectly. No digital trail. No cloud storage. No metadata that can be traced or hacked or used against us. Just a synthetic plastic sheet that can be burned to nothing, disappearing like smoke and leaving no evidence of atrocities that happen in rooms, just like this. Aurelio is in the office down the hall. No doubt with a pen scratching against paper with precision as he meticulously prepares the files that will accompany these photos; the thought makes my skin crawl and my stomach turn. It's a rule from the old guard. Everything must be paper, a rule that Gabe is utilising to burn it all to the ground; one photograph at a time.

A few months ago, this was just a job. A cold, hard transaction. I was the muscle, the unblinking observer, who didn't ask questions and didn't care about the answers. I was a tool, a weapon, a thing without conscience or feeling. I didn't care about the girls. I didn't care about their stories, their tears or their pleas for mercy. They were cargo, inventory, nothing more than a line item in a ledger. But then came Alba. Gabe's Alba. The girl he'd loved since they were kids; the one he'd talked about when we were young, stupid and thought we'd have normal lives. We found out she'd been snatched and pushed through his father's disgusting system; a betrayal by his father's most trusted man, so profound that it shattered something fundamental in Gabe. The rage that transformed his face when he found out is something I'll never forget, something that's burnt into my memory like a brand. He killed the man. It hadn't been nearly enough, but it is all he could do. Alba is safe now, tucked away at Gabe's house, where she is protected, loved and slowly healing from the horrors she endured; but the damage is done. The scales have fallen from his eyes, and now he's on a warpath, a quiet, simmering crusade to dismantle this part of the business from the inside out. It's a dangerous undertaking, needing a slow and steady demolition from the inside because the tendrils of this network are wrapped around some of the most dangerous men in the country, men who will kill without hesitation if they find out what Gabe is doing.

He stands across from me, his face a mask of stone while his jaw clenches so tight, I can see the muscle working beneath his skin. He hates every second. I can see it in the way his fingers grip the camera, in the way his shoulders are held rigid, in the way his eyes are empty, cold and utterly devoid of humanity. He's performing, playing the part of a man without a conscience, and he's doing it so well. If I didn't know him, if I hadn't grown up with him, if I hadn't seen the moment his heart broke, I'd believe it. But I do know him. I know the man beneath the mask. But watching him suffer like this, watching him do the one thing he hates the most in the world is starting to even affect me, starting to crack the ice that I've built around myself for so long; but, the only way to dismantle it all is from within.

He calls one of the girls forward. She stumbles, her thin dress doing little to hide the trembling of her limbs as her whole-body shakes with terror and desperation. Sobs wrack her body, pathetic little hiccups of sound that echo in the silence of the room, bouncing off the walls and coming back to us like accusations. Her eyes are red and swollen from crying, her makeup smeared down her face in dark rivulets, and there's a bruise on her arm that's already turning purple. She's young, too young, and the thought of what she's been through, what she's going to go through, makes something twist inside my chest.

"Please," she whispers, her voice cracking and breaking like glass. "Please, don't. Please, I'll do anything. I'll, I'll be good. I'll cooperate. Just please don't, "

Gabe doesn't flinch. His gaze is cold and empty; a void that swallows light. He raises the camera with a mechanical precision that speaks of repetition, of having to have done this over and over until it has become second nature. "Name."

The word is a shard of ice, sharp and cutting. Not a

question, but a command. An order. The kind of order that demands obedience, that brokers no argument or hesitation. The girl chokes on another sob, her eyes wide with terror as she looks at him, at me and then at the closed door behind us. She's looking for a saviour that isn't here; a rescue that will never come. Her lips tremble as she tries to speak, and I can see her gathering herself, trying to find the courage to defy him, but it crumbles before it even forms.

"Name," he repeats, his voice lowering this time with a growl that promises consequences; a tone that promises pain and suffering if she doesn't comply. It's a tone I've heard him use before, a tone that makes even me feel the weight of his displeasure.

"L-Lily," she stutters out, her voice barely audible. "My name is Lily."

The camera flashes, a brilliant, blinding white that erases her for a second, washing out the colour from the room and leaving only stark shadows and light. The whirring sound of the Polaroid spitting out the image is obscenely mechanical and cold in the quiet room, the sound of her humanity being reduced to nothing but a photograph on a piece of paper and a number in a file. Gabe plucks the photo from the camera without looking at it, his hand already gesturing for the next girl. He doesn't look at Lily as she's pulled back into the line by one of the other men; her face a mess of tears, snot and despair. He just waits, his finger on the trigger.

Ready to document the next tragedy.

Ready for the next ghost.

Chapter 2

Posey

The rage is a living thing inside me; a hot, molten core in the centre of my chest that the drugs can't touch; no matter how hard they try to drown it. It burns through the fog in my head like a beacon, a single point of clarity and fire within the disorienting haze that they've pumped into my veins over the past few days. My limbs feel heavy, disconnected almost, like they belong to someone else entirely, like I'm piloting a body made of lead and cotton; but the anger… the anger is all mine. It's a bitter, familiar friend, the only thing my father ever gave me that was truly my own; the only inheritance that matters. It's the thing that keeps me breathing when every-thing else wants to shut down.

I stand in a line of women; all of us trembling inside a damp, foul-smelling room that reeks of desperation and broken dreams. My eyes scan the women around me, their faces a blur of tear-streaked makeup and hollowed-out despair, their bodies thin and fragile in ways that mine will never be. Most of them are Asian, their delicate features drawn tight with terror, their eyes empty of hope. I seem to be the only white woman here, a fact that feels strangely significant; like I'm a different kind of product on the shelf; a novelty item that might fetch a higher price. The thought sends another wave of fury through me, so potent it makes my stomach churn with bile and rage, almost causing me to throw up.

I can feel the other women's eyes on me, like they are wondering what I'm doing here, how someone like me ended up in a place like this. They don't know that I'm stronger than they are, that my body is a weapon, or that I've spent my entire life training to be exactly that. They don't know that my father built me this way, piece by piece, day by day, with his fists and his demands and his endless, relentless expectations. They don't know that I should be unbreakable. And yet here I am, just like them. Waiting to be sold.

Sold. Like cattle. Like property. Like a thing with no value beyond what someone else is willing to pay for it. My own father, the man who was supposed to protect me, who was supposed to love me unconditionally, sold me. He's a kingpin in France, or so he likes to think; a small-time Napoleon ruling over a pathetic empire of drugs, weapons and broken lives. He built his reputation on violence and fear; on the backs of men who were too stupid or too desperate to know better. And now, using his own daughter. What a load of fucking shit. What a perfect, beautiful, infuriating load of shit.

He raised me to be his strength, in a voice smooth as silk he explained his plans for me. Daily training sessions of MMA and boxing that would leave my knuckles raw, bleeding and my body a canvas of bruises that bloomed in shades of purple, yellow and sickly green. I was seven years old the first time he put on the gloves and taught me how to throw a punch. I was eight when he made me spar with boys twice my size. By the time I was ten, I could take down a man twice my weight. By fifteen, I was nearly unbeatable in the ring. He pushed me, honed me, made me sharp, dangerous and lethal. Every morning before school, we'd be in the gym. Every evening after dinner, we'd be back there again. He never let me rest, never let me stop, never let me believe that I was anything less than perfect.

But he never let me compete. That was the thing that should have tipped me off, the thing I was too young and too desperate for his approval to understand. I begged him to let me fight in tournaments, to let me test myself against other fighters, so I could prove that I was as good as he said I was. He always refused. Just need you strong enough to defend yourself, he'd claim, his hand ruffling my hair in a gesture that felt like a benediction. That's all you need, mon amour. That's all that matters. I need you strong, but not too strong. I need you capable, but not too capable. I need you to be able to fight, but not to win.

I was too naive to understand what he meant. Too young to see the calculation in his eyes, the way he was measuring me like a piece of meat at market. He was training me to be a commodity, a product with a particular set of specifications. Strong enough to be valuable. Skilled enough to be interesting. But not so skilled that I could escape or fight my way free. It was a masterclass in control, a slow, methodical breaking of my spirit disguised as love and training.

The memory of that night plays on a loop in my mind, sharp and brutal through the chemical fog that clouds my thoughts. His men, the faces I've known my whole life, men who'd watched me train since I was a child, coming into my room without knocking. The rough hands grabbing me, my screams swallowed by the plush carpets of our home, by the thick walls that had been soundproofed to keep the noise of my training from disturbing the neighbours. I fought. God, how I fought. I kicked and screamed and clawed, landing a few satisfying blows that left marks; some that even made them bleed. I felt the crack of my fist connecting with someone's nose, heard the satisfying crunch of bone breaking. I managed to get one of them in a chokehold, his face turning purple, his hands scrabbling at my arms. For a moment, I thought I might actually escape. For a moment, I thought my training had been enough.

But there were too many of them. They were bigger, heavier, and they didn't care if they hurt me. They overpowered me through sheer numbers and brutality, a knee to my ribs that stole my breath; the sharp, searing pain making me gasp and falter. A fist connected with my jaw, sending me into a starburst of blackness that swallowed everything. I remember the taste of blood in my mouth, the feeling of my body going limp, the sensation of being lifted and carried like a sack of grain. I remember the sound of my father's voice, calm and measured, telling them to be careful not to damage the merchandise too much.

I woke up on a private plane, the hum of the engines a low thrum against my skull that made my head pound with a dull, relentless ache. My hands and feet were bound with zip ties that cut into my skin so tight that they drew blood, and the world was a woozy, swimming mess. I'd been drugged so high I couldn't have walked if I'd tried, my body a dead weight, my mind a swamp of confusion and pain. I drifted in and out of consciousness, unable to tell if hours or days were passing. There were faces above me sometimes, guards checking on me, making sure I was still breathing. There was the taste of water forced down my throat, the sting of needles in my arm as they kept me sedated, ensuring I remain compliant and unable to fight back.

And now I'm here. Melbourne, I think one of the guards had said during a moment of clarity, his Australian accent thick and unfamiliar. A world away from everything I've ever known, waiting to be sold to the highest bidder. Waiting to be broken by someone new, someone who will take all the strength my father built into me and use it against me; twisting it into something ugly and wrong.

A rough hand shoves me forward, breaking me from my thoughts, and I stumble, my legs still uncooperative, my body still heavy with the remnants of the drugs. I find myself standing in front of a man in a perfectly tailored suit. His dark hair is styled with a precision that seems out of place in this grimy hellhole, every strand in perfect order, and his eyes, a startlingly clear blue, are as cold and empty as a winter sky. He looks at me, his gaze clinical and assessing, like he's evaluating a piece of livestock at an auction. He's handsome, I suppose, in a sterile and untouchable way, the kind of handsome that belongs in magazines and boardrooms; not in a room like this. His face is sharp, angular, with high cheekbones and a strong jaw, but there's no warmth in it, no humanity. He's a statue carved from ice.

He opens his mouth, and the sound of his voice is a low command, smooth and controlled, the kind of voice that's used to being obeyed.

"Name?"

My rage, which had been simmering beneath the surface, boils over in an instant. The audacity. The sheer, unmitigated gall. Like I'm simply an object to be catalogued, a thing without a name or a history or a right to refuse. Like I'm not a person. I gather the saliva in my mouth, thick and foul from the drugs, and I spit. It lands squarely on his cheek, a gob of defiance that I hope stings, that I hope humiliates him the way he's trying to humiliate me. For a moment, there's a flicker of something, maybe surprise, maybe even a flash of anger in those blue eyes, but it's gone as quickly as it came, swallowed back down into that icy void.

He slowly pulls a pristine white linen handkerchief from his pocket, and wipes my spit from his face. His movements are deliberately measured, controlled, like he's performing a ritual. He doesn't look angry. He just looks… disappointed. Like I'm a child who's misbehaved, and he's deciding whether I'm worth the effort of disciplining.

"Name?" he repeats, his voice even colder this time, a spoken word that somehow carries more weight than a shout.

The drugs are still swirling in my system, making me slightly groggy, causing the world tilt on its axis, and my thoughts to be sluggish and slow. But my name is my own. It's one of the few things I have left, one of the few pieces of myself that they haven't been able to take. My mother gave me my name before she died, before my father decided to remake me in his image. Posey. A flower. Delicate and pretty and utterly useless in his world. It's the last piece of her that I carry with me, and I'll be damned if I don't claim it now.

I lift my chin, my voice a low, gravelly rasp; rough from screaming and the drugs.

"Posey Hudson."

A bright white flash blinds me, erasing the world for a moment, before the whirring sound of a camera makes me flinch. He took my picture. Another piece of me stolen, reduced to a square of paper, a number in a file, a commodity with a price tag. Before I can react, before I can spit again or kick or do anything else to fight back, I'm being pulled away, dragged to the other side of the room where another man is waiting. And then I see him.

He is, without a doubt, the most beautiful thing I have ever seen. Not handsome like the man in the suit, but beautiful in a way that's dangerous, feral and utterly wrong. He's massive, at least six-foot-four, with a body built of pure, hard muscle that is straining against the fabric of his black button-up shirt. The sleeves are rolled up to his elbows, revealing forearms covered in a tapestry of black ink; tattoos that snake up his forearms in intricately well detailed designs. A mix of symbols and images I can't quite make out through the fog in my head, but they're beautiful in a dark, twisted way. The tattoos disappear under his sleeves, and I wonder how far they go, how much of his body is covered in the dark artwork. He's wearing black slacks that fit him perfectly, and his hair is dark, neat and short, not quite a buzz cut, but close. He's leaning against the wall, like he's not even trying and yet he's still the most dangerous thing in the room; an image of casual menace.

As I'm shoved towards him, the corner of his mouth lifts slightly upwards in a ghost of a smile that doesn't reach his eyes. He tilts his head to the left, studying me with an intensity that makes my skin prickle, and his dark eyes are unreadable as they rake over me from head to toe. It's not a leer, not exactly. It's more like he's cataloguing me, taking inventory, but there's something else in his gaze too, something I can't quite name. Something that makes my breath catch in my throat.

The man holding my arm leans over saying something to him, his voice a low murmur that I can barely hear over the pounding of my own heart. "She is going to auction."

The beautiful man, my mind aptly names 'the grim reaper' because there's something about him that speaks of death and darkness, pushes off the wall with a fluid grace that seems impossible for someone so large. He doesn't speak. He just reaches out, his large, calloused hand closing around my upper arm, before he pulls me away from the other guard. His grip is firm, unyielding, but there's a strange lack of brutality in it. It's not the rough, painful grip the men who dragged me here had.

It's ... possessive.

Chapter 3

Catcher

My gaze fixes on her as one of the hired grunts shoves her in my direction, and the moment she stumbles forward, something inside me shifts. It's subtle, barely perceptible, but it's there. She catches herself with a surprising stability, her body adjusting to the momentum with a grace that speaks of training, of muscle memory and of someone who knows how to move. The action confuses me, before I realise that it's what sets her apart from the sea of broken women that I've spent the last hour cataloguing and reducing down to photographs and paperwork.

I take her in, my eyes tracing the lines of her as she stands before me, defiant even in her drugged and dishevelled state. Her hair is a rich, dark brown that falls around her shoulders in a tangled mess. It's matted in places where blood has dried from the injuries on her head. There's a strand of it caught across her face, and I have to resist the urge to reach out and brush it away. Her skin is porcelain, so pale that it looks like it hasn't seen the sun in years, making the angry red marks on her arms and the dark bruise blooming on her jaw, sharp and brutally evident. The bruise is the colour of storm clouds, a mix of purple and black with sickly yellowing at the edges; it speaks of the violence and struggle of someone who fought back. The thought sends a surge of something dark through me.

Her eyes, the same deep brown as her hair, are wide and filled with a potent mixture of fear and undiluted fury. They're not the same empty, vacant eyes as the other women; the ones who've already surrendered, who've already accepted their fate. These eyes are alive. They're burning with a fire that hasn't been extinguished, that can't be extinguished. They're the eyes of someone who's still fighting, still defiant, still refusing to break. Looking into them is like staring into the sun, and I find myself unable to look away.

But it's her body that holds my attention, sending a jolt of something unfamiliar and deeply unsettling through me. She's not the typical kind of woman that ends up in this place; all soft curves and fragile bones specifically chosen to appeal to the basest desires of men. No, she looks strong. Built; her shoulders broader than most, with a defined line of muscle that speaks of strength and dedicated training, of hours spent honing her body into a weapon. It's the kind of build I see on fighters, on women who know how to handle themselves, who've spent their lives learning how to not only throw a punch, but take one too. Can she fight? The question hangs in my mind, a puzzle I desperately want to solve, a mystery that's suddenly become the most important thing in the world.

Her clothing, clings to her frame, revealing the architecture of her body in a way that's both infuriating and intoxicating. Her visible thighs are slender but corded with muscle, the kind of muscle that comes from repetition and discipline. There's not an ounce of softness to her, not a single place where she's been allowed to be weak. This is not the body of a victim. This is the body of a warrior, and the realisation sends my blood pressure spiking.

I feel my jaw tightening, my fists clenching at my sides as I take in every detail of her. Despite her defiant expression, the way her chest rises and falls slightly too fast with each breath betrays her fear,. The way her hands are curled into fists shows she's ready to fight at a moment's notice. The way her legs are positioned, her body balanced, like she could move in any direction. She's been trained. Someone has spent time teaching her how to fight, how to move, how to survive. The thought makes my dick twitch.

The guard who shoved her towards me grunts, his voice a low gravelly sound that grates on my nerves like nails on a chalkboard. His breath smells like stale beer and cigarettes, and his eyes are fixed on her with a hunger that makes my blood boil. "She's going to auction," he says, the words casual, like he's commenting on the weather.

The words make me pause. A twisting sensation hits my gut, one that I've never felt in all my years doing this job. Auction. This woman, with her fighter's body and burning eyes, is going to be sold to the highest bidder. Put on a stage, paraded around like a prize sow, and handed over to some depraved bastard who will take pleasure in breaking her. The thought is so repulsive, so utterly wrong, that it makes my blood run cold and then hot again as I cycle through a range of emotions I don't have names for; feelings I don't know well. A protective and possessive rage that coils in my stomach like a snake, tightening around my organs, making it hard to breathe. I've never cared before. Not once in all the years I've been doing this. Not for any of the women I've seen pass through this warehouse or for any of the horrors I've witnessed and participated in.

Before I can even process the thought, before I can examine this new and dangerous feeling, my body moves, acting on an instinct I didn't know it possessed. My arm snakes out, my hand wrapping around her upper arm. The skin is soft and warm, but beneath it, the muscle is hard and unyielding; just as I suspected. It's like touching steel wrapped in silk, the sensation sending a jolt of electricity through me. I pull her into me and away from the guard, my body shielding hers from his leering gaze. She's shorter than me, maybe five-foot-ten to my six-foot-six, but she fits against my side perfectly, her head coming to rest just under my chin. I can feel the heat of her body and the slight tremor that runs through it. The scent radiating off her is not the cheap, cloying perfume the other women wear, but something else, something else entirely that lays beneath the grime.

She stiffens at my touch, her body going rigid, every muscle tensing as if preparing for an attack. For a moment, I think she's going to fight me, and I almost hope she does. I want to feel her strength, to test myself against her, to see if she's as formidable an opponent as her body suggests. But instead she speaks, her voice a low husky rasp, laced with an unmistakably French accent.

"Fucking grim reaper."

The words are a curse; an insult dripping with disdain and fury. But they send a jolt of something that feels dangerously like pleasure through me, a sensation that's equal parts arousal and admiration. She's not broken. She's not even close. She's a fighter, through and through, and I find myself wanting to see more of her fire, spirit, and raw unbridled defiance. I want to know what she looks like when she's fighting for real, not when she's drugged and disoriented. I want to know if she can actually fight, or if her body is just the result of some genetic lottery win.

A smirk tugs at the corner of my mouth, a genuine, unbidden reaction that surprises me. I can't remember the last time I smiled at something that wasn't cruel or mocking. "That's me," I murmur, my voice a low rumble that's meant to be reassuring but probably just sounds menacing. I tighten my grip on her arm, not enough to hurt, but enough to let her know that she's not going anywhere. she's mine now, at least for the moment.

I turn and march her down the corridor, away from the main room, away from the prying eyes and the stench of despair that clings to every brick and beam of this place. There are two types of holding cells here: the large, open pens for the women who are sold in bulk to brothels; and the individual cells for the ones who are deemed special enough for auction. The ones who are considered too valuable to be lumped in with the common stock and who will fetch a higher price.

As we walk, I can feel her struggling against my grip, testing my strength in an attempt to gauge whether she can break free. The thought sends a thrill through me. It's clear she's not giving up. She's not accepting her fate. She's still fighting; still trying; still hoping that she can escape. It's foolish, given the circumstances, but it's also beautiful in a way I don't know how to explain.

The corridor is dimly lit, with only a few flickering fluorescent lights casting harsh shadows on the walls. Our footsteps echo in the silence, a rhythmic sound that seems to mark time, to mark the passage from one moment to the next. I can feel her heart racing through where arm presses against my ribs and I can hear her breathing. It's slightly ragged and slightly too fast; betraying her fear despite her defiant actions. She's afraid, but she's not showing it, not really. She's keeping it locked down, compartmentalised, controlled. It's impressive.

I stop in front of one of the single cells; a small, concrete box with a heavy steel door that's been painted a dull, institutional grey. It's a cage, plain and simple, and the thought of putting her into it feels wrong.

I remove the keys hanging from my belt, the metal cold against my fingers as I unlock the door. The industrial lock is heavy, designed to keep people in, not out. The door swings open with a groan of protesting metal, revealing the sparse interior of the cell. There's a cot with a thin mattress, a toilet in the corner, and nothing else. It's a cell designed for temporary holding, not comfort.

I give her a gentle push inside, and she stumbles, catching herself on the wall with her hands. She turns to face me immediately, her brown eyes blazing with a hatred so pure, it's almost beautiful. There's no fear in her gaze now, only fury, defiance, and a burning need to hurt me the way she's been hurt.

I close the door and slide the bolt home; the heavy clang echoing throughout the silence of the corridor like a death knell. "There is a spot in hell with your name on it, reaper," she says, her voice low and steady, each word a perfectly aimed dart, each syllable dripping with venom.

A slow smile spreads across my face, and I lean closer to the door, my voice dropping to a conspiratorial whisper that only she can hear. "Oh, I know, little bird," I note, the nickname that slips off my tongue suiting her perfectly, after all she is just a caged little bird now. "I'll get there when it's my time."

I turn away from her cell, the image of her face, a furious, beautiful mask of defiance, burnt into the back of my eyelids as if seared there by a branding iron. As I walk back down the corridor the echo of the heavy steel door slamming shut seems to follow me, a final, definitive sound that separates her cell from the rest of this waking nightmare.

I return to the main room, having to make a conscious effort to ensure my movements become more mechanical and to detach my mind from the tasks ahead; that woman has made something stir that I thought was impossible. I force the cold numbness back into place, a familiar cloak I've worn for years. The air still thick with fear, but the sharp edge of it is now dulled by exhaustion and resignation. It's a different kind of terror now, a quiet, hopeless despair that's almost worse than the frantic panic from before. Three more women are designated for auction, their files marked with a small, almost imperceptible symbol that seals their fate. I take them one by one, my grip firm but impersonal, my face a blank mask of indifference. It's a performance, and I am the lead actor.

They don't fight. They don't spit. They don't call me the fucking grim reaper. They just follow, their bodies trembling and their eyes vacant and hollow; souls already gone from this world. They are ghosts in their own skin. I place each one in her own concrete box, the sound of the bolts sliding home a grim, repetitive rhythm that echoes the soulless beat of my own heart. Every clang a nail in a coffin; another sin on my already tallied out existence. With each door I lock, the image of Posey's blazing eyes flashes in my mind.

The rest of them, a dozen or more, are herded into the larger cell at the end of the hall. They huddle together in a mass of shivering bodies and quiet sobs, their individual identities already beginning to fade as they merge into one singular entity of suffering.

With the women secured, I head to the office, the room a jarring shift back into reality. The office is clean and modern, with a solid desk and expensive chairs. Gabe is already at the desk, his suit jacket slung over the back of his chair, his tie loosened and a half-empty glass of whiskey in his hand. He looks tired, the weight of what we're doing now etched into the lines around his eyes, a deep-seated exhaustion that no amount of sleep will cure. Aurelio sits at the desk, his face illuminated by the cold, blue glow of his computer screen, even though his work, the real paperwork containing the manifestation of these women's lives, is stacked neatly in front of him.

For the next two hours, we work in a heavy, oppressive silence; broken only by the rustle of paper and the soft click of a pen. My job is to take the Polaroids, one by one, and attach them to the corresponding files. Its a mindless, soul-crushing task, a descent into a paper-based hell. Each photo is a life reduced to a glossy square of synthetic paper, a face that will haunt my dreams like a ghost. I keep my expression neutral. But my eyes are scanning every file, my heart thumping a low, anxious rhythm as I search for one name, one face.

And then I find it. Her photo is on top of a thin file, the stark white flash of the camera bleached the colour from her face, but it can't erase the fury in her eyes. If anything, it makes it more pronounced. It's a terrible picture, but it's her; a mugshot of a fallen angel. My fingers tremble slightly as I pick it up, the glossy surface cool against my skin. Beneath it, the file is thin, just a single sheet of paper that details the transaction of a human life. I find myself reading it, my breath catching in my throat.

Posey Hudson. 23 years old. From France. The details are sparse, clinical, but they paint a picture of unimaginable betrayal. Her father, some small-town crime boss with an inflated sense of self-importance, is asking for one million euros for her. A million euros. For his own daughter. The words swim before my eyes. He isn't just selling her; he's put a price tag on her head, a number that in his eyes represents her worth. The thought is so monstrous, it's almost incomprehensible. I wonder if he'd be pissed off if he doesn't get the money. The question sparks an idea, a dangerous, reckless idea that takes root in my mind, beginning to grow with a speed that is both terrifying and exhilarating. Ideas I've never had before, thoughts that don't belong to the man I've always been, the man who just follows orders.

My mother's voice, a soft, gentle echo from a lifetime ago, whispers in my memory. I'm a teenager again, sitting beside her bed in the white sterile room that smelled of antiseptic and death. She was so thin, a fragile bird with broken wings, but her eyes were still bright, still full of love. "One day, Catcher," she'd said as she stroked my head, her hand all bone and paper-thin skin, "You will meet a woman, and she will make you question everything. She will tear down the walls you've built around your heart and make you feel again. It will be terrifying. And when it happens, you are to keep her safe. For she will be yours."

I'd dismissed it at the time, nothing but the sentimental ramblings of a dying woman, a fairy tale to make a grieving boy feel better. But now, looking at this picture, at her name, the words come rushing back with the force of a prophecy on it's way to being fulfilled. Posey's done that. In the space of a single encounter, she's made me question, made me feel something other than the numb indifference that has been my constant companion for years. So now she's mine, right?

When the last file is stamped and stacked, Gabe lets out a long weary sigh. "Dinner?" he asks, running a hand through his perfectly styled hair, messing it up for the first time all night. "Alba's making pasta."

Aurelio nods without looking up from his screen, his focus absolute. "Yes. I'm starving."

They both look at me, waiting for my answer. The old me, the Catcher from yesterday, would have said yes without a second thought. I would have gone to Gabe's, eaten Alba's food, and pretended that we were just three friends having dinner, not three men who just processed human beings like cattle. But the man I am now has other plans. "No," I answer, my voice rougher than I intend. "I've got four fights lined up this fortnight. Need to train."

Gabe frowns, a look of genuine concern on his face. "I really do wish you would quit that shit, man. You're going to get yourself killed in that ring one of these days."

I just grin, a cold, sharp smile that doesn't reach my eyes, a predator's smile. "It's not my time yet, brother."

He just rolls his eyes, a gesture of fond exasperation that we've shared a thousand times. "Fine. Have fun training." He and Aurelio head for the door, their footsteps echoing in the quiet office. I wait, counting the seconds, my body thrumming with a nervous energy I haven't felt in years. I listen until I hear the sound of their car starting, the engine a low growl that fades into the distance, leaving me alone in the belly of the beast.

Then I move. I walk back down the corridor, my footsteps silent on the concrete floor, my heart pounding with a mixture of fear and exhilaration that makes me feel more alive than I have in a decade. I stop in front of her cell, the sound of my own breathing loud in the silence. I slide the bolt back, the sound a deafening crack in the quiet, before I pull the heavy door open.

She's sitting on the edge of the cot, her back ramrod straight, her hands resting on her knees. She looks up at me, her eyes wary, guarded, but the fire is still there, banked low but ready to roar to life. She's ready for a fight. She's ready for anything. The thought sends a thrill of admiration through me that is so strong it's almost painful.

I hold out my hand, my palm open in a gesture of peace, an offering, a surrender. "I give you two choices," I state, my voice low and steady. "Leave with me, or stay."

Her eyes narrow, searching my face for some sign of deception, some hidden trap. She doesn't trust me. She has no reason to. "What are you going to do to me?" she asks, her voice a low, suspicious whisper, her French accent making the words sound both elegant and dangerous.

I take a step closer, my hand still outstretched, my gaze locked with hers, willing her to see the truth in my eyes, the truth I'm only just beginning to understand myself. "Nothing," I answer, my voice dropping even lower in a raw and honest promise.

"Nothing you won't ask for."

Chapter 4

Posey

It's been two weeks.

Fourteen days since I'd made a choice in the echoing silence of the concrete hellhole he had placed me in. Two weeks ago, I looked into the eyes of the man I dubbed 'the grim reaper' and saw something other than cold, hard death; I saw a choice. It wasn't a choice at all, not really. Leave with him or stay. Staying meant the auction, a fate worse than any I could imagine. Leaving with him was a leap into the unknown, a step into a different kind of darkness, but it was a step forward.

So, I took his hand.

His skin was rough, calloused, but his grip was surprisingly gentle as he led me out of the warehouse into the cool night air. The scent of leather and cologne overwhelmed me as he placed me in his overly expensive SUV. We drove for what felt like hours, leaving the city lights of Melbourne behind, plunging deeper and deeper into the Australian bush. Up until that day, I'd never been out of France before, and the darkness outside the window was absolute, filled with the strange, alien like sounds filling a foreign world I was yet to understand. Choruses of clicks, chirps, and screeches; a symphony of the night, that just set my teeth on edge.

He took me home. The word, a bitter irony that feels wrong on my tongue. But as we pulled up the long, gravel driveway, I couldn't deny the strange beauty of the place. At the end of the drive sat a large, two-story building made of deep red brick, with stately white columns supporting a porch that wraps around the entire structure. It looks like something out of an old movie, a place of quiet solitude and sanctuary. But I know better. It's a prison, not a home. A cage is still a cage, no matter how gilded.

The last few days I've learnt the Australian heat is a new kind of beast; a dry, oppressive weight that settles on you the moment you step outside. It's nothing like the gentle warmth of a French summer. This sun is angry, relentless. The entire property is surrounded by a silver fence, an iron monstrosity that you couldn't possibly climb because it's so high that it seems to scrape the sky. The top is crowned with a tangle of wicked-looking barbed wire; glinting in the sunlight like a row of sharp teeth. The gate is electric, a solid wall of steel that only opens with a pin code. The property is a fortress, designed to keep the world out, and me in.

Trust me, I've tried to escape. On the very first day, fuelled by a desperate, frantic energy, I tested my prison. I found a spot at the back of the property, hidden from the house by a thicket of strange, spiky trees, and I tried to climb the fence. The moment my hands made contact with the metal, a jolt of electricity shot through me, so powerful it threw me backwards onto the dry, dusty ground. It hurt like a bitch, a sharp, searing pain that left my muscles twitching and the palms of my hands covered in small, angry red welts. Defeated but not broken, I spent the rest of the day walking the perimeter, searching for any weakness, any flaws in the security. I found nothing but the relentless, baking sun. By the time dusk began to settle, my pale skin was a painful fiery shade of red, and I was so dehydrated I could barely stand.

Catcher had come home to find me collapsed on the porch steps in a miserable, sun-scorched heap. He didn't say a word. He just disappeared inside and came back a moment later, tossing a plastic bottle at my feet, filled with a clear, cooling gel. Aloe vera, the label said. "Put it on your burns," he'd grunted, his voice devoid of emotion as he walked past me into the house. The gel was nice; a soothing balm on my tortured skin, but I didn't thank him for it. I wouldn't give him the satisfaction.

Every day since has been the same. Like clockwork, he leaves for work in the early morning; a silent imposing figure disappearing down the long driveway. Before he goes, he always says the same thing. "There's food in the fridge." And there always is. The fridge is stocked with freshly cooked meals in containers. A range of simple, hearty foods like roast chicken, pasta, and salads. It's another one of his confusing contradictions. He's my captor, but he cares for me and feeds me in a strange, detached way.

The room he'd allocated me is on the second floor. It's a plain sterile space that only houses a bed and a bedside table. There are no personal touches, no decorations, nothing to make it feel like anything other than a holding cell. For the first few days, I was on edge, my body coiled tight with anticipation as I waited for him to come into my room at night. I Waited for him to claim the prize he'd stolen. But he never did. He never even opened my door. He sleeps in a room at the opposite end of the hall, and most nights I fall asleep to the faint, rhythmic thud of him hitting the punching bag on the porch.

After the sunburn faded, leaving behind a light tan, I'd taken to sitting out in the sun daily, just for a few minutes at a time, forcing my skin to get used to the new, harsher environment. The house is so far out in the bush that I never see other cars or other people. The only sign of life is the wildlife, and they are things of nightmares. Strange birds that laugh like madmen, spiders the size of my hand, and kangaroos that watch me with a disconcerting intelligence from the edge of the woods. It's a beautiful, terrifying world.

Two days in, he'd brought me four bags of clothes. He just dropped them on the bed, his expression unreadable. "I hope they fit," he said, his voice rough, and then he'd left. I've wondered if he picked them out himself, if he'd walked through shops thinking about what I might wear or what would suit me. The thought sent something warm and confusing through my chest, and I quickly buried it.

The clothes were all simple, practical. Leggings, shorts, bike shorts, singlet tops, t-shirts, and a few jumpers. What the fuck he thought I needed jumpers for, I will never know. It was nearly forty degrees every single day; a relentless and oppressive heat that made me want to shed my own skin. I was always too hot, always sweating, always uncomfortable. The jumpers seemed like a cruel joke, or perhaps a sign of how little he actually understood about me. But most of the clothes fit perfectly, as if he'd somehow known my exact measurements. A few items were a little small, but the majority were right. He'd also gotten me underwear; it's been the only time I've really wanted to say thank you. Because not wearing any underwear isn't for me at all. The freedom of it was nice, sure, but there is something about having that basic layer of protection, that small sense of dignity that matters more than I want to admit.

There are certain products I really want for the bathroom, things I need, but I've been too scared to ask for anything. In fact, I haven't said much to him at all really. We've existed in this strange, silent dance of two people sharing a house but barely acknowledging each other's presence. He leaves for work each morning, and I am left alone with my thoughts and the endless, suffocating heat.

Now, after fourteen days, I am bored. The initial terror has faded, replaced by a restless, simmering frustration that's starting to eat me alive from the inside out. My body aches for movement, for the familiar burn of exertion, the release of a good workout. My father may have trained me for his own sick purposes, but he'd also given me an addiction, a need for a release that only fighting seems to provide. It's a hunger that grows stronger with each passing day, a primal need that can't be ignored.

Catcher has training equipment scattered all over the porch. A punching bag hangs from a thick wooden beam, so old and worn that it's held together with what looks like a hundred layers of duct tape. The tape is peeling in places, revealing the sand-filled interior beneath. There are worn leather gloves and hand wraps tossed on a bench nearby, and I can see the indentations in the leather where his hands have gripped them countless times. Every time I walk past it, I can feel it calling to me like a siren song; the rough texture of the wraps, the satisfying thud of my fist hitting the bag, the sweat, the burn and the sweet, sweet exhaustion. I want to use it. I need to use it. But I'm not sure if it's allowed.

But the boredom is an ache, and the punching bag is starting to look like the only cure.

Fuck it. It's been two weeks. If he was going to hurt me, he would have done it by now, right? I'm not sure. I can't get a read on this grim reaper, can't figure out what he wants from me, what his endgame is. But I'm tired of being afraid. I'm tired of being bored. I'm tired of being trapped in this limbo between captivity and something that almost feels like care.

I walk out onto the porch, my bare feet warming against the sun-soaked wood. The heat surrounding me like I've walked into a sauna. I pick up the hand wraps, my fingers trembling slightly as I begin to wrap my hands. The motion is muscle memory, something my body knows how to do even when my mind is screaming at me to stop. I wrap carefully, creating a tight, supportive base for my knuckles. The wraps are worn, soft from years of use, and they smell like him, that same masculine scent that filled his SUV.

Once my hands are wrapped, I begin my regular routine. A warm-up to stretch my muscles, loosening my joints. Then I begin to move, my body finding its rhythm. I do sprints from the porch to the fence line and back, my legs burning with the effort, my lungs working hard in the oppressive heat. It feels good. It feels so fucking good. I feel good, the best I have felt in weeks. The exertion a release, like a valve opening to let out all the pressure, frustration and fear that's been building inside me.

But even as I'm moving, as I'm finding that release, my mind is working; there has to be a way out of this place, right? There has to be some weakness in the security, a flaw I haven't found yet. And if there is, where do I go from here? I can't go home to France. My father would just sell me again, handing me over to the next highest bidder without a second thought. But I have nothing in this country. No friends, no family, no connections. I'm completely alone in this vast, strange land.

I lose myself to my thoughts, my body moving on autopilot, until I hear his voice, cutting through the afternoon heat like a sharp and unexpected blade.

"You lean on your right side too much. You need to tighten your core more."

I jump, my entire body going rigid, my heart leaping into my throat. I spin around, my fists still raised, ready to fight. He's standing at the edge of the porch, his massive frame silhouetted against the bright afternoon sun.

Chapter 5

Catcher

I stand in the shadow of the house, my body hidden by the deep shade of the porch overhang, watching her. I've been watching her for a while now; my truck parked silently at the edge of the tree line where she wouldn't see it. I'd wondered how long it would take. For two weeks, the punching bag has hung there, a silent invitation, and for two weeks, she's ignored it. A part of me, the dark cynical part, had started to doubt myself. I was so sure she was a fighter, so certain that the body she inhabited was indeed a weapon. But a sliver of disappointment had begun to creep in as the days passed. Maybe I'd been wrong. Maybe, I'd just seen what I wanted to see.

But now, standing here, watching her move, I know I wasn't wrong. She's magnificent. Her body is a symphony of controlled power; each movement fluid and precise. She moves with a grace that is both beautiful and deadly, her muscles flexing and releasing in a rhythm that is as hypnotic as a heartbeat. The fury on her face as she trains, the sheer, unadulterated rage she pours into every punch and kick, is astonishing. The fucking woman is stunning. She's a storm, a hurricane, a force of nature; and I am a man who has spent his entire life chasing storms.

I get a stiffy every time her dark angry eyes meet mine. It's been like this since the moment I brought her home; a constant aching hardness, that is both a pleasure and a torment. She's under my skin, ingrained into my body; like a fever I can't sweat out. And it's causing problems.

Gabe had been fucking furious about me taking her. He and Aurelio had cornered me the next day, their faces a mixture of anger and concern. They'd given me so much shit, their voices low and urgent in the confines of Gabe's office. They wanted me to just pay for her, to send the one million euros to her bastard of a father so it was all dealt with. A clean and simple business transaction. But I refused. The word had come out of my mouth before I'd even had a chance to think about it. No. I will never pay for a wife.

Fuck. Why had I thought that? Why had the word, wife, sprung into my mind, fully formed and terrifyingly real? I'd instantly pushed the thought away, burying it deep, but it keeps resurfacing at the most inconvenient times. She's not my wife. She's just... mine. That's all it is. A simple truth. She belongs to me now. I stole her, and I'm not giving her back.

Her fighting routine is good. Very good, actually. Her form is clean, her punches sharp, her kicks powerful. She's been trained well, that much is obvious. But there are a few things she's lacking, small imperfections that only a trained eye would notice. She leans on her right side too much, putting too much weight on it, leaving her left side vulnerable. It's a subtle flaw, but a dangerous one. Why had no one corrected it? Whoever trained her was either lazy or stupid, and the thought of someone being so careless with her makes my blood boil.

I watch her for a few more minutes, my eyes tracing the lines of her body as she moves, the sweat glistens on her skin as her breath comes in short, sharp gasps. She's lost in the moment, her mind focused solely on the motions, she doesn't hear me approach. I step out of the shadows and onto the porch; my boots making no sound on the sun-warmed wood.

"You lean on your right side too much," I say, my voice cutting through the afternoon heat. "You need to tighten your core more."

She jumps, her entire body going rigid, a startled gasp escaping her lips. She spins around, her fists still raised, her eyes wide with a mixture of fear and anger. The look of fury on her face, the way her chest heaves with each ragged breath, the fire in her eyes, it's the most beautiful thing I've ever seen. It takes everything in me not to cross the distance between us and kiss her until we're both breathless.

"You scared the shit out of me," she snarls, her voice a low, dangerous growl.

I hold up my hands in a gesture of surrender, a slow smile spreading across my face. "I'm sorry," I say, meaning it; I didn't mean to scare her. I just... wanted to talk to her. "I didn't mean to scare you."

Her eyes narrow, her suspicion a palpable thing between us. "How long have you been there?"

"Awhile," I admit, my gaze dropping to her wrapped

hands and then back to her face. "I wanted to see your form. It's good, you know. Needs a little tweaking, but very good."

She frowns at that, a flicker of something, possibly pride, or annoyance in her eyes. She looks down at the dirty worn wraps that belong to me, and a flush of colour rises in her cheeks. "Sorry," she mutters, her voice barely a whisper. "I just grabbed what was here."

I brush it off with a wave of my hand, taking a step closer to her. "No, no," I say, my voice softer than I intend. "You're welcome to use it all. I'll get you some more wraps, your own pair." The thought of her using my things, of her hands being where mine have been, sends another jolt of pleasure through me. "In fact," I continue, the words tumbling out before I can stop them, "you can do anything you want within the fence line."

It's a test. An offering. A declaration. I'm giving her freedom, a strange, twisted kind of freedom, but freedom, nonetheless. I'm telling her that this is her space now, too. That she is not just a prisoner here.

She looks at me, her head tilted as her eyes search my face for the catch; some sort of trick, a lie. She doesn't trust me. She has no reason to. But there's a flicker of curiosity and hope in her gaze, too. It's a dangerous combination.

"Are you my master now?" she asks, her voice low and sharp.

A growl escapes my chest. "No," I say, my voice rough with an emotion I can't quite explain. "Never call me that. I'm not one of them. I will never be one of them."

She tilts her head, her eyes narrowing, and I can see

the wheels turning behind those dark, intelligent eyes. "But you are a part of it," she says, her voice quick and sharp, cutting through my denial like a blade. "And you took me, which means I'm yours now."

The words hit me like a punch, and not in a good way. Coming from her mouth like this, it sounds wrong. It sounds twisted, dark and exactly like the kind of thing the men who buy women would say. It sounds like something I would have said a month ago, without hesitation. The realisation makes my skin crawl.

"No," I say, my voice firm, absolute. "You're not mine in that sense. I didn't buy you. I took you out of there because I could. Because I wanted to."

She steps closer, her wrapped hands clenching into fists, her eyes blazing with a righteous anger that I deserve. "You're still a part of it," she says, her voice dripping with accusation. "What type of human buys and sells women?"

The question lands like a grenade; the explosion reverberating through my entire body. I feel the disgust in my own gut, a sick churning sensation that makes me want to vomit. I've spent so long compartmentalising, separating the man I am from the things I do, but she's forcing me to confront it all. She's forcing me to look at myself and see the monster staring back.

"Me," I say, the word bitter on my tongue. "That's who. A man who does what he is told. A man who follows orders and doesn't ask questions. But I'm also a man who is helping the future owner dismantle the whole thing."

Her eyes widen, shock registering across her face. "Dismantle?" she asks, her voice barely a whisper.

"Yes," I confirm, my jaw clenching. "Dismantle. We're

taking it apart, piece by piece, from the inside out. But these things take time. They take patience. And they take men like me, willing to do the dirty work; willing to be the villain in someone else's story."

She opens her mouth, as if to respond, but I cut her off before she can speak; I can't have this conversation right now. I can't stand here and justify myself, can't explain the impossible moral calculus that has become my life. It's too much. She's too much.

"Tighten your core when you throw a punch from the right," I say. "You're leaving yourself open on the left side. It's a weakness."

She blinks, clearly thrown by the abrupt change in subject, but she nods slowly. "Okay," she says, her voice small.

"I have to work tonight," I tell her, turning away before I do something stupid; like pull her into my arms and promise her things I can't deliver. "I'll be home late. I just came home to grab my bag."

I turn on my heels, walking away from her as my heart pounds in my chest. I stride into the house, heading straight for my room and grab my bag; my movements sharp and jerky because I'm pissed off with myself. As I pass her door on my way out, I pause, my hand hovering over the frame, and I think about her question.

What type of human buys and sells women?

Me. I am. Even though we're taking it apart, even though we're working to dismantle the whole operation from the inside; I am still that person. I've still done those things. I've still stood in rooms and watched women be reduced to photographs and paperwork. I've still been complicit in their suffering.

And for the first time in my life, I feel remorse. Real, bone-deep remorse that settles in my chest like a brick; a crushing weight of guilt that makes it hard to breathe. I grip the doorframe, my knuckles white, I'm still part of the problem, and I will be part of it till it's gone. It's a bitter pill to swallow.

I walk down the stairs and out to my car, the echo of my footsteps a hollow sound in the vast emptiness of the house. The front door clicks shut behind me, a sound of finality that does nothing to silence the voice in my head. *What type of human buys and sells women?* Her question following me; a relentless accusation that I can't outrun. I get into the SUV, the familiar scent of leather doing nothing to soothe the storm raging inside me. I start the engine, the powerful roar a welcome distraction, and I drive. I watch the gate close behind me in the rearview mirror, an iron maw shutting me out of the strange sanctuary I've created, and I push the accelerator to the floor.

I need to fight tonight. The need is an ache, a gnawing hunger in the pit of my stomach. I'm so mad at myself, at the man I am, and the things I've done. The guilt and remorse is a poison in my veins, and the only antidote I know is violence. The 45 minute drive to the underground fight club is a blur of speed and darkness, the trees lining the road nothing but a smudge of green in my peripheral.

I park the SUV in my designated spot; a small perk Gabe gave me after I bitched relentlessly about having to park half a mile away from the entrance. The club is in the basement of a nondescript warehouse in an industrial part of the city, a place that doesn't officially exist on any map or in any official records. It's a ghost, just like the men who fight here. I get out and head inside, the thumping bass of the music vibrating through my chest and rattling my bones. The smell is strong, a mix of sweat, stale beer and the metallic tang of blood. It's a familiar, almost comforting assault on my senses, the scent of a place where men come to shed their humanity and become something else entirely.

I bypass the main floor, where the sea of faces are illuminated by harsh strobe lights. They're a blur of flesh and teeth and hunger, all of them here to watch men destroy each other for money and glory. The roar of the crowd is a constant, deafening backdrop; a white noise of human depravity. I push through the throng, my massive frame parting the crowd like water, and head straight for the changing room.

The room is small, grimy, and smells of liniment and unwashed bodies, of tape and sweat and the ghost of a thousand fights. The walls are concrete, stained with blood and God knows what else. There's a row of old battered lockers lining one wall, and a single bench in the centre of the room. My movements become mechanical as I strip out of my clothes, and pull on my fighting shorts. The fabric has worn thin from years of use; soft and supple like a second skin that I've inhabited so many times it feels more natural than my own body. I wrap my hands, the rough canvas creating a tight, supportive base for my knuckles. The motion is meditative, grounding in a way.

I'm cracking my neck, trying to loosen the tension in my shoulders, working through the knots of muscle that have accumulated from the stress of the day, when Gabe walks in. He takes one look at my face and his expression shifts, his perfectly styled eyebrows furrowing in concern.

"What's got your knickers in a twist?" he asks, his tone light, but his eyes are serious.

"Nothing," I grunt, my voice a low growl.

Gabe smiles, a knowing, infuriating smile that makes me want to punch him. "Trouble at home? Is your mail-order bride not washing your jocks?"

I shake my head in a sharp, angry movement. "Shut the fuck up, Gabe."

He just chuckles, leaning against the lockers, his arms crossed over his chest. "She not slotting into the shoes you want? Not playing the part of the grateful little captive?"

His words are a deliberate provocation, hitting their mark. I turn to face him, my fists clenching at my sides. "Honestly," I say, the word raw and honest as it tears from my throat, "I have no idea what the fuck I'm doing."

The admission hangs in the air between us, a rare moment of vulnerability that silences Gabe's teasing. He sobers instantly, his expression softening. "Do you want to know why you didn't get shot for taking her, Catcher?" he asks, his voice quiet.

I look at him, my curiosity piqued despite my anger. "Why?"

"Because it's the first time ever that I've seen you interested in something other than killing," he says, his gaze steady and unwavering. "The first time I've seen you give a single fuck about another human being. I thought... I thought maybe she might be the one to save your soul."

I shake my head, a bitter laugh escaping my lips. "I don't have one of those."

"Yes, you do," Gabe insists, his voice firm. "We all do. And you deserve to be happy, you miserable bastard." He pushes off the lockers and walks out, leaving me alone with his words, with the impossible, ridiculous hope he's just dumped at my feet.

I stare after him, my mind reeling. Save my soul. The idea is so absurd it's almost funny. I shake my whole body, like a dog shaking off water, trying to dislodge the uncomfortable weight of his words. I push my mouthguard in and walk out to the ring.

The roar of the crowd is a deafening wave of sound, a tsunami of human bloodlust that crashes over me and fills my lungs. It's intoxicating, a surge of adrenaline that courses through my veins like liquid fire, making my heart pound in my chest like a caged animal desperate to escape. Gabe is on the other side of the cage, his expression unreadable, Aurelio standing next to him like a shadow, his face a mask of calm indifference. I step into the ring, the canvas soft and slightly tacky beneath my bare feet, the texture a reminder of all the blood that's been spilled here over the years. I meet my opponent's gaze, and I can see the calculation in his eyes, the assessment he's making. He's big, bigger than me, with a face that looks like it's been rearranged more than once by someone who wasn't particularly gentle about it. His nose is crooked, his left eye slightly smaller than his right, a roadmap of violence written across his features in scars and asymmetry. So many men step into the ring with me, their eyes full of bravado and misplaced confidence, their bodies tense with the certainty that they'll be the one to finally take me down. Yet none of them walk out. Not a single one.

The fight starts slow, a cautious circling, a testing of boundaries. We're two predators assessing each other, looking for weakness, for an opening, for the moment when we can strike. A few small exploratory punches are thrown, feeling out the other's speed and power. A couple of kicks are thrown and easily blocked, our movements economical, controlled, conserving energy. It's a dance, an ancient ritual, a prelude to the violence to come. And then it's on. Something inside me snaps, a switch flips deep in my brain and my mind goes blank. The killing lust takes over, a red haze that descends over my vision like a curtain being drawn, and I smile. This is where I feel like myself. This is where I'm allowed to show the crazy, the darkness that I keep locked away in the depths of my mind. This is where I'm allowed to let out all the rage, the guilt and the self-loathing that threatens to consume me from the inside out. This is my church, and violence is my confession, my prayer, my absolution.

It's a brutal round. I move with a speed and ferocity that takes him by surprise. I'm a whirlwind of fists and feet, each blow landing with a sickening thud that echoes through the cage and reverberates through the crowd. He's strong, I'll give him that, but I'm faster, meaner, and more willing to do whatever it takes to win. I break his nose with a vicious elbow strike, the crunch of bone a satisfying sound that sends a jolt of pleasure through me. Blood pours down his face, obscuring his vision, and he stumbles backward as his hands come up to protect his face. I press my advantage, moving in for the kill. I shatter his ribs with a powerful kick, the impact so forceful that I feel the bones give way beneath my foot, a sickening crunch that speaks of a serious life-threatening injury. A pained grunt escapes his lips, a sound of pure agony as his body betrays him, and he drops to one knee. I'm on top of him in an instant, my fists a blur of motion, each punch a release, a purging of the poison from my veins. I punch his face into the canvas, again and again and again, my knuckles connect with his skull, making a wet meaty sound that makes my blood sing. The rage is a roaring inferno in my body, a wildfire that consumes everything in its path, leaving nothing but ash and destruction in its wake. The crowd is a distant, faceless roar. Their bloodlust feeds my own, as their screams and cheers become a soundtrack to my violence.

I don't stop until there's nothing left to hit, until his face is an unrecognisable pulp of blood, bone and tissue. His body goes limp beneath me, his breathing shallow and irregular; the death rattle of a man whose time has come. I feel a sharp, searing pain in my hand and I look down to see that I've cut it open, a deep gash across my knuckles where a piece of his shattered skull sliced through my wraps like a razor blade. Grey brain matter is smeared across the canvas in a grotesque pattern. The obscene sight should sicken me, should make me feel something, but I am utterly devoid of humanity at this point. I get off him, my chest heaving from exertion, my body slick with sweat and his blood. The ref rushes in and checks for a pulse. There isn't one. He pronounces the man dead, his voice steady despite the horror of what he's just witnessed. I don't feel a thing. No remorse, no guilt, no satisfaction.

Just a hollow, empty calm; a void where my emotions should be.

I walk out of the ring, the cheers of the crowd fading into a dull buzz. Gabe meets me back in the change room, his face a mixture of pride and concern. Aurelio walks in a moment later with the first aid kit, his movements efficient and precise as he stitches up my hand and glues the split above my eyebrow. The sting of the antiseptic a welcome, grounding pain.

"You know," Gabe says, his voice quiet as Aurelio finishes his work, "I thought having Posey, you might want to give this up."

I frown, the question genuinely confusing to me. "Why the fuck would I do that?"

Gabe just looks at me, his expression unreadable as he asks the one question I have no answer for.

"Who the fuck is going to look after her if you're dead?"

Chapter 6

Posey

I wake up to the unfamiliar sensation of a body that feels both exhausted and alive. Every muscle aches; a deep, satisfying soreness that reminds me I'm still here, still capable. The training session yesterday was the answer to a question I didn't even know how to ask. It was a release, a purging of the restless energy and simmering rage that had been coiling in my gut for two long weeks. My body aches in all the right places, a testament to the work I put in, and for the first time since I was stolen from my life, my mind isn't a chaotic whirlwind of fear and anger. It's quiet. The relentless noise has subsided, and I'm able to think more clearly, to see things with a sharpness that had been missing.

I swing my legs out of bed, the wooden floor cool beneath my feet, and make my way to the kitchen. The house is silent, bathed in the soft, grey light of early morning. I find a cup, a bowl, a packet of instant oats, and a tea bag, my movements slow and deliberate in the quiet. As I fill the kettle, my mind drifts back to Catcher's admission from yesterday. Dismantle.

They were trying to get rid of the human trafficking side of the business. The words echo in my memory, a strange, discordant note in the symphony of my assumptions about him. Why? Why would a man like him, a man who is so clearly embedded in that world, want to tear it down? Was he just talking shit, feeding me a line to make me more compliant? But if he was, why say it at all? He doesn't come across as someone who just says things for the fun of it. Every word he's spoken to me, as sparse as they have been, have felt deliberate, weighted. But I've only known him for two weeks. That's not enough time to know anyone, especially not a man as complex and contradictory as the grim reaper.

The microwave beeps, and I pull out the steaming bowl of oats; the simple, bland smell filling the kitchen. I pour the hot water over my tea bag, watching the water slowly turn a rich, amber colour. I'm so lost in my thoughts and the puzzle that is Catcher, that I don't hear him enter. Not a creak of the floorboards, not the whisper of his breath. Nothing. Not a single sound.

I turn to leave the kitchen with my cup of tea in one hand, the bowl of oats in the other, only to nearly jump out of my skin. He's just... there. Standing in the doorway, a silent, towering shadow. And he looks like hell. A fresh cut slices through his left eyebrow, held together with a faint, shiny line of what looks like surgical glue. His bottom lip is split and swollen; a dark angry purple against the pale skin of his face. And his right hand, the one not braced against the doorframe, is heavily bandaged with clean white gauze wrapped tightly around his knuckles.

A startled gasp escapes my lips, my body reacting to his sudden apparition and his battered appearance all at once. My body jerks slightly, the hot tea sloshing over the rim of the cup and scalding my hand. I cry out, a sharp, involuntary sound, as the cup slips from my grasp.

Before it can hit the floor, he's moving; a blur of motion, covering the distance between us in a single and fluid stride, despite what must be an aching body. He snatches the cup from the air with his uninjured hand, his reflexes impossibly fast, and sets it on the counter. Then his bandaged hand is on my arm, his touch surprisingly gentle, as he pulls me towards the sink.

"You're like a bloody mouse, you know that?" he says, his voice a low, rough grumble as he turns on the water and guides my hand beneath the stream. "Jump and run at every bloody sound."

The cool water is a shock, a blessed relief on my burning skin. I stare at his hand, the clean white bandage is stark against his tanned skin. I can see a faint red stain seeping through the gauze, a ghost of the violence that put it there. He was out all night. He comes home looking like he's gone ten rounds with a monster, and now he's tending to my minor burn with a gentleness that feels completely at odds with the man who's earnt such injuries.

"You don't make sound," I say, my voice barely a whisper, my eyes still fixed on his hand. "That's the problem."

He looks at me, his dark eyes searching my face. "What?"

"You pop up all over the place," I explain, my heart still hammering against my ribs from the shock of seeing him. "And I never hear you coming."

A low chuckle rumbles in his chest, a sound so unexpected it makes me look up, my gaze meeting his. The movement pulls at the cut on his lip, and he winces slightly. "You think I'm stealthy?" he asks, a ghost of a smile playing on his lips despite the pain.

And then it happens. A flutter. A strange, unfamiliar sensation in the pit of my stomach, like a thousand tiny butterflies have suddenly taken flight. His chuckle is deep and rich, a sound that vibrates through me, and I find myself wanting to hear it again, even if it causes him pain. It's the first time I've heard him make a sound that isn't a grunt, a command, or growl.

"Yes, I think you're stealthy," I say, my voice steadier now, though my heart is still racing. "You would have to be in your line of business."

The words land like a rock in still water, the lighter mood evaporating instantly. I watch as his expression shifts, the ghost of a smile fading from his face. He grabs a tea towel from the counter and gently dries my hand; his touch careful and deliberate. He examines the red mark, his dark eyes studying it with an intensity that makes me feel exposed.

"You'll be okay," he says, his voice low and measured. "Thankful that tea wasn't hotter. It looks a bit sore, but you should be fine."

He moves away from me and grabs a cloth, crouching down to clean up the spill on the floor. Even crouched down, he still comes up to my belly. He's a mountain of a man, all hard muscle and controlled power, and watching him clean up after me, seeing him perform a mundane, domestic task, does something strange to my insides. I want to reach down and touch his face. I want to run my fingers over the cut on his eyebrow, trace the line of his split lip. Fuck, where did that thought come from? What the fuck is wrong with me? He's my captor. He stole me from my life and locked me in a cage, even if that cage has started to feel less like a prison and more like a sanctuary.

I walk to the table and sit down, pulling the bowl of oats toward me. I need the distance. I need to put space between us before I do something stupid. I watch him finish cleaning, watch him straighten up and move with the careful precision of someone who is hurting but trying not to show it.

"Why are you so banged up today?" I ask, my voice carefully neutral. "And why do you always seem to have a bruise or a swollen face?"

He leans against the counter, his bandaged hand resting on the edge. "I had a fight last night," he says simply. "A good one, too. He managed to get a few hits in. I've had a few this last fortnight, but none of them really managed to do any damage. Last night was a good one though."

I stare at him, my spoon pausing halfway to my mouth. "You fight?"

"Yes," he confirms, his gaze steady on mine. "Underground fight club. I do it most nights when I'm not working."

The words hang in the air, and suddenly I'm remembering the underground fight clubs in France, the ones my father used to take me to. The roar of the crowd, the smell of blood and sweat, the primal violence of it all. My father loved to bet on the fights, loved the thrill of watching men destroy each other for money and glory. As much as I wanted to be in a real fight one day, to test myself against another fighter, I've never wanted to be in one that ended in death.

"So, to the death then?" I ask, my voice barely a whisper.

He smiles, a sad, knowing smile. "Yes. To the death."

I feel the blood drain from my face. I think of the bandages on his hand, the cut on his face, and I realise that he's a killer. Not just in the abstract sense, not just as part of his job in the mafia, but in the most literally visceral way possible. He kills men with his bare hands for sport.

"How long have you been fighting for?" I ask, needing to understand this man, needing to know what I'm dealing with.

He thinks for a moment, his gaze distant, as if he's looking back through years of violence and blood. "I think I've always fought, in some way," he says slowly. "But my first underground one was when I was sixteen. My father took me. He thought it would help to stave off some of my anger." He pauses, and I can see the pain flicker across his face, a shadow of old grief. "My mother died when I was a teen, and I took up brawling to help with the grief. My dad helped me channel it into more structured fighting. It was the first time I felt normal again, so I've been this way since."

I stare at him, my oats forgotten. His mother died when he was young. He's been killing since he was a teenager. He's been channelling his rage into violence for more than a decade. The picture that is the grim reaper becomes a little clearer, but it's also a little more complicated. He's not just a monster. He's a man who was broken and found a way to survive, even if that way is through violence.

"Sixteen," I repeat, the word tasting strange on my tongue. "You killed at sixteen."

"Yes," he says, his voice matter of fact; as if discussing the weather. "In my world, that's actually quite old."

I raise my eyebrow, processing this information. Just ask the fucking question, Posey. Just ask.

"What is your world?" I say, my voice steady despite the trembling in my chest. "Will you explain it?"

Chapter 7

Catcher

"Fuck, Yeh alright," I say, my voice steady despite the turmoil churning inside me like a storm at sea. "But let me make you another tea first. How do you take it?"

"White with one sugar," she says, and I nod, moving to the kettle with deliberate ease.

As I prepare the tea, my mind becomes a battlefield. How does one explain an entire world of darkness and violence to someone who's already been victimised by it? My mother's words echo in my head, a constant loop that's been playing on repeat since the moment Posey came into my life. *She will be the one. And when it happens, you are to keep her safe.* But what does that mean? Does it mean there should be no lies? Does it mean I have to lay bare every sin, every crime, every moment of complicity?

I think of Gabe and Alba. He tells her everything, every detail of what we do, who we are. She's a part of this whole thing now; whether she wanted to be or not. Felix has Aurora, and she's involved in this world as well, although not as deep as Alba. And then there's Matteo and Eleanor, he brought her into this world as his queen from day one. Thinking about it, my father used to say, honesty is the best policy. But it leaves me wondering; what if that honesty could get me killed one day? What if not being completely honest gets her killed?

The thought instantly makes me feel a ill, a sickening twist in my gut that forces me to confront the reality of the situation. I can't protect her if she doesn't understand the world that she's now a part of. I can't keep her safe if she doesn't know the dangers, the rules, the hierarchy.

I quickly make her a new tea and one for myself, the familiar ritual grounding me as the kettle steams and the water turns a rich, amber colour. Grabbing both cups, I take a seat across from her, the table a barrier between us, and I take a breath. This is it. This is the moment where I either tell her the truth or continue to hide behind the walls I've built. I choose the truth, even if it destroys me.

"I need to start at the start," I say, my voice low and measured, each word carefully chosen.

"Okay," she says, taking a sip of her tea. She hums, a small sound of satisfaction that sends a jolt of pleasure through me. "You make a nice tea."

I smile, a real smile, and it steadies me more than I want to admit. "Thank you."

I take a moment to gather my thoughts, finding the right words to explain a world that's been my entire existence; a world that shapes every choice I make and every line I cross. "Years ago, four young boys migrated with their families to Australia from Italy; Sydney to be exact," I begin, my gaze fixed on hers. "One of them was the son of a man who was part of the mafia in Naples. His father was trained in a world that didn't exist here in Australia, so when they moved, his son saw an opportunity."

I pause, taking a sip of my tea, watching her face as she processes this information. She's listening intently, her brown eyes focused on me, and I can see the intelligence there, the way she's already starting to piece things together, to understand the scope of what I'm about to reveal.

"So, he rallied the other three boys, and together they created what is called the Four Seats," I continue, my voice steady but heavy with the weight of history. "When they became adults, they expanded. They started with drug rings and weapon exports. Ricci and Moretti ran Sydney together, Rossi moved to the Gold Coast to run Brisbane, and Gallo took over Melbourne. It just expanded from there, like a cancer spreading through the body of the country. What started as drugs and weapons expanded into business, restaurants, strip clubs, brothels, trafficking, and information. All of it interconnected, all of it feeding into the machine."

The word trafficking hangs in the air between us like a curse, and I see her flinch slightly, her fingers tightening around her teacup. I press on, because stopping now would be worse than continuing, it would be a betrayal of the honesty I'm trying to offer her.

"About twelve years ago, there was a massive war in Sydney," I continue, my voice harder now, edged with the violence of that time. "A rival group tried to take over. They didn't win, but the Ricci's were killed. Their son, Matteo, became head of the Four Seats overnight. He was young, but a lot of things started to change when he took over. He channelled a lot into legitimate business, mainly nightclubs and strip joints. He still sells drugs and weapons, but nothing to the scale that the Rossi's do in Queensland."

I lean back in my chair, watching her process this information, seeing the way her mind is working behind those intelligent eyes. "Since then, Enzo Moretti was killed. He'd turned on the group because he didn't like the way things were heading, didn't want to evolve. He also betrayed Matteo, so he was put down by the heads of the Four Seats. A message, you understand. You don't betray the family."

It was brutal but it needed to happen. Enzo was like a cancer, one who let power take over and chose to betray them all.

"Now the old men are handing down the reins to their sons, one by one," I continue, my voice steady but tinged with something that might be regret. "Gabriel Gallo's father handed his seat off to him two weeks ago. That's how I was able to take you without being killed. Aurelio and I are Gabe's right-hand men. Growing up we've been his best friends. Our own fathers worked for Gabe's father; so naturally when he took over, he appointed us as the second in charge."

I pause, gathering my thoughts, preparing to explain the catalyst for everything that's changed. "Months ago, we were out celebrating Gabe's birthday and the fact that his dad was handing the seat to him. We were at one of our clubs, when we came across a woman." I watch Posey's face carefully as I speak, seeing the way she's processing this. "Her name is Alba. She had been Gabe's high school sweetheart. She had been missing for years. None of us knew where she was or what had happened to her. Her father told Gabe she'd abandoned the family and run off. But the truth was far darker than that."

I take a sip of my tea, the warmth grounding me as I continue. "Her father had sold her into the trafficking side of the business. He sold her to Gabe's father's right-hand man, he took her and sold her off without Gabe's father even knowing. If he'd known, he never would have allowed it. Gabe and Alba were the type that were meant to be. The Gallo family loved her. She was always supposed to be part of their world, not a commodity to be bought and sold."

The pain in my voice is genuine, the memory of that night still raw. "When the truth came out, Gabe pulled her from that world. He had to buy her off her owner at the time, which was a mess because Alba thought he wanted her like a sex slave. But he had to buy her to get her out. There was no other way. Once he explained everything to her, that she was actually free, that he loved her and always had, she finally understood. Those two are soul-mates, Posey. They're inseparable now."

I lean forward, my elbows on the table. "It's what really sparked the dismantling. Gabe had wanted to slow down the trafficking for years, but he didn't have the power to do it. Being in this position, taking over the seat, means that he can finally do something about it. Matteo is all on board with it. Antonio, the head of the Rossi seat, understands that we need to evolve to stay in power. He's handing his seat off to his twin sons soon, so that's going to be interesting to see. They make me seem sane."

I run a hand through my hair, a gesture of frustration. "But here's the thing, it's impossible to just chop the head off a hydra; it just sprouts more heads. We need to take over the brothels that aren't owned by us, because you can't sell a sex slave to a brothel when you're the owner, right? Which we've been doing. We've officially taken over five in the area. There are still nine more we don't own. Then we need to slow down the intake of women from overseas sales, until it's just a trickle."

I pause, thinking of Eleanor, of her radical vision for what could be. "Eleanor, Matteo's wife, she has ideas about this. She doesn't think we should stop it entirely. She thinks we should keep going, but instead of selling them as slaves, we actually give them what they came here for, a job, a house, a life. And if they want to be sold as wives, they can be. She says choice is key. I would rather see it gone completely, but I can also see what she means. Some women want to be sold as wives. As long as the man is nice enough to them and they're happy. Some don't want that life at all. They want to work, and we own a lot of businesses. Plenty of places for them to work. We could do it. We could actually give them a choice."

I watch her face as I explain this, waiting for her reaction, for her to understand that we're trying, in our own dark and complicated way, to make things better.

Chapter 8

Posey

I sit in silence for what feels like an eternity, my mind struggling to process the sheer magnitude of what Catcher has just revealed. The Four Seats. Years of organised crime spanning Australia. Drug rings, weapon exports, businesses, trafficking. It's a machine so massive, so intricate, that it makes my father's operation in France look like a child's game. My father, who I'd thought was powerful, he's a small-time player in comparison to this.

I grew up in a world of drugs, weapons, and gambling. I watched my father build his empire, watched him make deals and break men. But nothing, absolutely nothing, prepared me for the scope of what Catcher is describing. These men aren't just criminals. They're architects of an entire criminal infrastructure. They're dangerous in a way that goes beyond violence. They're dangerous because they're organised; they think strategically and they understand power, leverage and how to maintain control.

And they want to give the women choices.

I understand the logic of it, even as it twists something

inside me. If they stop the trafficking entirely, another organisation will step in and fill the void. They'll be worse, probably. Less organised, more brutal. By staying in power, by maintaining control, Catcher, Gabe and the others can dictate how things operate. They can ensure that women aren't just discarded, that they have some semblance of agency in their own lives. It's a dark kind of mercy, but it's a mercy, nonetheless.

I take another sip of my tea, the warmth grounding me as I organise my thoughts. "So does that mean you bought me?" I ask, my voice carefully neutral.

He stiffens slightly, and I see a flash of something dark cross his face. "No," he says firmly. "I refuse to pay for women. I won't do it."

I frown, confused. "So, you just took me?"

He grimaces, and I can see the conflict playing out across his features. "Aurelio paid for you because I refused," he says, the words coming out like they taste bad in his mouth.

"What?" I set my cup down carefully, processing this new information.

"Your father had to be paid," he explains, his jaw clenching. "And I refused to pay for you, so Aurelio paid so your father wouldn't cause us any trouble."

Aurelio paid for me. Catcher refused to pay for me. Which means... what? That he cares? That he sees me as something more than a commodity? Or is it just another layer of the game, another move on a chessboard that I don't fully understand?

I look at him across the table, at this massive, scarred man who kills for sport and works for the mafia, and I try to reconcile the violence I know he's capable of with the tenderness he's shown me. The tea he made me. The way he cared for my burned hand. The way he explained his entire world to me, laying himself bare in a way that must have cost him something.

"Why?" I ask, my voice barely a whisper. "Why did you refuse to pay for me?"

He leans back in his chair, and I can see him gathering his thoughts, preparing to reveal something that clearly matters to him. "I refuse to pay for women," he says slowly, his dark eyes fixed on mine with an intensity that makes my breath catch. "My mother, bless her soul, taught me a few things in her short life. She told me that under no circumstance do I force a woman or pay for one."

He pauses, and I can see the pain flicker across his face at the mention of his mother, a shadow of old grief softens his harsh features. "She knew what my father did for a living. She knew he worked in the same warehouse I do now. She knew what he did, and she still loved him every single day. She told me a lot of things before she died, and some have stuck with me." His voice drops lower, more vulnerable. "It doesn't mean I'm a saint. I've just never had to pay for a woman before."

I raise my eyebrow at him, processing this revelation. The image of him, this massive, scarred, violent man, being taught by his mother about respect and agency is jarring, almost impossible to reconcile with the killer I know he is. And then another thought creeps in, one that makes heat rise in my cheeks and my stomach twist with an emotion I don't want to name. *He's never had to pay for a woman before.* Which means women come to him willingly. Which means he's stunning, which he absolutely is, and women would flock to his side, would want him, would clamour for his attention. The thought provokes a strange, sharp feeling in my chest, a burning jealousy that I immediately try to stamp down. For God's sake, Posey, what the fuck is wrong with you? He's your captor. You should hate him, not fantasise about him.

He leans forward into my personal space, closing the distance between us, and my breath catches in my throat. His hand comes up slowly, deliberately, and runs down my cheek. His touch is surprisingly gentle for such a large, calloused hand, his fingers rough against my skin. The sensation sends a jolt of electricity through me, a spark igniting something deep in my core, and I find myself frozen, unable to move, unable to think, unable to do anything but feel.

"I bought you some stuff," he says, his voice low and rough, intimate in a way that makes my pulse race. "It's in the car. I'll go get it."

And then he's gone, pulling away and scurrying from me like a scared little mouse, leaving me sitting alone with my tea and my chaotic, spiralling thoughts.

I sit in the silence of the kitchen; the only sound is the soft clink of my cup being placed down on the table with trembling hands after I take another sip. My cheek still tingles where his hand touched me, the sensation lingering like a ghost, and I press my palm against it, trying to ground myself in reality. This man took me. He refused to pay for me, but he locked me up in his house. He explained about the entire criminal empire he's part of, and he did it with a honesty that felt almost sacred, like a confessional in church.

But what he said about Alba echoes in my mind, refusing to be ignored. Gabe bought her. He took her home. And Alba thought he wanted her as a sex slave, but he didn't. He wanted her free. Was Catcher doing the same to me? Was I free?

Then why the locking up in his house? That's not free, it's captivity, no matter how gentle he's been about it. It's control, no matter how much he claims to respect women.

Was there more to the story? Do I want to know? Would he let me go if I asked? Do I want to go?

I have no money, no passport and no way to leave this country. I can't go home to my father. He'll just resell me for more money, and that situation won't be like this one. Catcher might have locked me up, but he does provide for me here. He's made me tea, cared for my burn and He's explained his world to me like I matter. He's refused to pay for me, like I am worth more than a sum of money.

As long as he doesn't expect me to be his sex slave, I could survive like this. I could build something here, something that resembles a life.

But the idea of having sex with Catcher provokes strange feelings throughout my body, a heat spreads through me like wildfire. He's massive and powerful; a mountain of muscle. I imagine being under that mountain of man, his weight pressing me into the mattress with his large, scarred hands, touching me, exploring me, claiming me. The thought sends a jolt of arousal through me, heat pooling low in my abdomen, as I feel my cheeks flush with equal parts shame and desire.

But he's my captor, I should want to escape, shouldn't I? I should be planning my exit, not fantasising about what it would feel like to have him inside me, not wondering what his lips would taste like, not imagining the weight of him on top of me. What the fuck is wrong with me?

Fuck, I think the grim reaper is pretty. God's sake, Posey.

The sound of the front door opening pulls me from my spiralling thoughts. Catcher returns with a few bags in his massive hands, and he sets them on the table in front of me. "For you," he says simply.

I look inside the first bag and find it filled with gym gear; sports bras, leggings, tank tops, all in my size. The second bag is filled with dresses, beautiful dresses in soft colours and flowing fabrics that make my breath catch. They're elegant and feminine and nothing like anything I've ever owned. They're perfect.

I smile at them. "Thank you," I say, my voice soft.

He nods, and then adds, "I asked Alba to pick them up for you. She did a better job than I did the first time around."

I look up at him and I smile. "You did well the first time," I say, and I mean it.

He looks at me for a long moment, and I can see something shift in his expression, something softening inside of him. But before I can analyse it further, I ask the question that's been burning in my mind since he brought me here.

"Am I a prisoner here?" The words come out before I can stop them, raw and honest.

His deep, dark eyes stare into my face, searching for

something I'm not sure I have to give. "No," he says finally.

"So why am I locked up inside this place?" I press, my voice steady despite the trembling in my chest.

He takes a breath, and I can see him choosing his words carefully. "I just explained to you who I am, and who I work for," he says, his voice low and measured. "These walls keep you safe while I'm at work. They make sure nothing can harm you. I had the fence built when I bought this place so I could sleep without being paranoid, so I could relax for once and not worry that my past was after me."

I stare at him, processing this explanation. The walls aren't a cage. They're a sanctuary. They're protection. But they're also a prison.

"So, I can leave?" I ask, needing to hear him say it.

"With me, yes," he says. "You're not safe out there without me."

So, not a cage but a cage. Free but not free. Great.

I look down at the dresses, at the gym gear, at this man who's given me everything except the one thing that matters, the freedom to choose. And I realise that maybe, just maybe, that's the most honest thing about this entire situation. He's not pretending I'm free. He's not lying to me about what this is. He's keeping me safe, and in doing so, he's keeping me captive. It's a paradox I'm not sure I'll ever fully understand, but it's one I'm beginning to accept.

Chapter 9

Catcher

"I don't have to work today," I say to her, my voice steady despite the chaotic storm roiling inside me, it's been building for weeks. "I am going to go and train for a bit this morning."

I turn on my heel and leave the room before she can respond, before I do something stupid like pull her into my arms and kiss her until we're both breathless. God, all of it is too much. I told her the truth. She's the first person I have ever been honest with, the first person I've allowed to see behind the walls I've spent decades building, brick by brick, stone by stone. And even though it's liberating to be able to say everything you want and to lay yourself bare like that, it's terrifying to expose every dark corner of your soul. Absolutely fucking terrifying. My stomach has been doing somersaults since I explained my world to her, since I handed her those bags and watched her smile, watched her eyes light up with genuine pleasure at the dresses Alba had picked out.

Gabe handed the bags off to me last night after the

fight, his eyebrow raised so high it nearly disappeared into his hairline. He'd had to spare six guards for Alba to go shopping for me, six men pulled from their duties to escort his wife to the shops, just so she could pick out dresses for my captive. He hadn't really asked about it, hadn't demanded an explanation, just that one sly comment last night about *Who will look after Posey if I die*. I'm not going to die, so it isn't relevant. But also, it's gotten under my skin, burrowing deep, like a splinter I can't remove, like poison slowly spreading through my veins. There are four more fights booked over the next four weeks. Four. I'm going to have to make sure I live through them all. I've never been scared to walk into the ring, never hesitated, never questioned whether I'd make it out alive. The ring has always been my sanctuary, my church, my place of absolution. But fucking Gabe has planted a seed with his casual comment, and now it's growing, spreading roots through my mind like a weed, beginning to choke out every rational thought.

I walk straight out to the bag on the back veranda, the morning sun already hot on my bare skin, and grab the wraps. The familiar motion grounds me, centring me, reminding me of who I am and what I'm capable of. I stretch, getting my muscles loose and ready, as I try to shake off this random feeling of butterflies and knots in my gut. They need to fuck off. I just need a moment to stamp it all back down, to lock away the vulnerability, the fear and the desperate, consuming need to keep her safe, to keep her here, to keep her mine.

I start my warm-up, slowly getting lost in the bag. The thump, thump, thump of my fists connecting with the heavy canvas is a rhythm I know intimately, a meditation that's been my salvation since I was sixteen years old. The sound is hypnotic, the exertion a release that's more powerful than any drug. Gradually, my mind begins to quiet. The noise fades. The anxiety recedes. The obsession with her retreats to the back of my mind, at least for the moment. There's only the bag, my fists, and the burning in my muscles as I push myself harder and faster. Sweat pours down my face and chest, soaking into the waistband of my shorts, and I lose myself in the violence of it all.

I have no idea how long I've been training, lost in the zone where nothing else exists, where time becomes meaningless and there's only the present moment, when a flash of colour catches my eye. Yellow. Bright, vibrant, and impossible to ignore, kind of yellow. My head turns that way instinctively, my body responding before my mind can catch up, and I see her.

Posey is walking across the yard in a stunning butter yellow dress, the fabric flowing around her like water, like silk, like a second skin. She's dragged one of the chairs from inside, all the way outside to sit on, and she moves with a grace and power that steals my breath and makes my heart skip a beat. She walks like a fighter, her shoulders thrown back with confidence, her long, toned legs eating up the distance with each purposeful stride. I can see the muscles ripple across her back, the dress cut so low in the back that it shows off the defined lines of her shoulders, spine and the curve of her lower back. She's a work of art, a masterpiece of strength, beauty and danger, and I want to run my finger down her spine, to trace every muscle, every scar, and every inch of her.

I stop my movement, my fists dropping to my sides as I just watch her. I can't move. I can't breathe. I can't do anything but watch as she settles into the chair, crossing her legs with a fluid grace, and she looks out at the property, at the trees, the sky and the vast emptiness of the bushland. She looks peaceful. She looks serene. She looks free, even though I know she's not. Even though I know these walls are a cage, no matter how much I try to convince myself they're a sanctuary, a place of safety and protection.

My dick lengthens in my shorts, hardening with a speed that's almost painful. The sight of her, the way she moves, the way the yellow dress clings to her curves and then flows away, leaving her back bare, it's too much. It's overwhelming. I palm myself, trying to stop the response, trying to regain control of my body, but it's a losing battle. She's under my skin, in my blood, buried in my body like a fever I can't sweat out, an infection that's spreading through every part of me.

I watch her for a long moment, committing every detail to memory. The way her hair falls down her back in waves, the colour like dark chocolate in the sunlight. The curve of her neck, the delicate line of her collarbone. The strength in her shoulders, the power in her back. The way she sits, poised and alert, like she's ready to fight or flee at a moment's notice. She's beautiful, but it's more than that. She's dangerous; a threat to my sanity and my control.

And I want her more than I've ever wanted anything in my life. More than I've wanted to fight. More than I've wanted to kill. More than I've wanted to breathe.

I give up. I can't do this. I can't stand here and pretend

that training will help, that exertion will burn away this obsession, this need, this desperate hunger that's consuming me from the inside, out. This woman has buried herself so deep inside me, and it's only been a few weeks. Weeks. And yet, I can't stop thinking about her, wanting to taste her, wanting to claim her in every way possible. Why is it that now, after all this time, a woman can turn my thoughts to chaos?

I storm back inside, my movements sharp and jerky, my body tense and aching with need, my shorts barely containing my hard dick as I head up the stairs to my room. I unwrap my hands with rough, impatient movements, the tape falling away to reveal the raw, bruised skin beneath, fresh blood drips from the cut on my hand. I strip from my shorts and walk into my bathroom.

I look at my reflection in the mirror, and I see a man I barely recognise. My whole body is a canvas of tattoos, intricate designs that tell the story of my life, my pain, my rage, my losses. There are skulls and roses, crosses and daggers, names of the dead and symbols of power. There isn't a lot of space left, only my two ring fingers on each hand, and a small section on one of my legs. Tattoos have always been a release for me, a way to channel my emotions when I can't fuck or fight them out, when the violence inside me needs an outlet. But where do you ink when there is no skin left? Where do you put the pain when every inch of your body is already marked, already claimed by the darkness?

I look down at my still hard dick, now weeping with pre-cum; the clear fluid glistening in the bathroom light. I grip it tightly in my hand, my fingers wrapping around the shaft, and I squeeze, making myself growl at my own reflection. The sound is low and dangerous, the sound of a predator, and it echoes off the tile walls. Fuck, I want her. I really want her. I have since I first saw her, since that moment in the warehouse when she spat on Gabe and called me the grim reaper. She can take what I give. I can see it in the way she moves, the way she trains, the way she carries herself with such strength and defiance. Her body is strong, built for endurance and power, built to take everything I have to give. I won't crush her. She's perfect for me.

My hand starts to work myself up and down, the motion slow and deliberate at first, savouring every sensation. I hiss at the feeling, using my thumb to spread the pre-cum over the tip and back down, going slow, savouring the building pleasure like it's a fine wine. In my mind, I picture her in that fucking butter yellow dress, the way it clung to her body like a second skin, the way her back was exposed and vulnerable to the world. I imagine slowly pulling that dress off her, deliberately revealing inch after inch of her toned, muscular skin. I imagine running my hands over her shoulders and down her spine, before gripping her hips as I pull her against me, as I make her understand that she belongs to me.

My hand moves faster now, my breathing becoming ragged and harsh, my chest heaving with exertion. The pleasure builds, a wave of heat that spreads through my entire body like wildfire, consuming everything in its path. I'm close, so fucking close, and all I can think about is her. Her dark eyes, and that long brown hair; perfect to twist around my hand and pull.

"Fuck," I growl, my release hitting me out of nowhere. My cum spills over my hand and onto the marble counter, as I continue to pump and pump. I grip the edge of the sink, my body shaking with the force of my orgasm, my muscles trembling from the intensity of it. I stare at my reflection, my chest heaving and my jaw clenched tight.

I need her. Not just physically, though. God knows she's consuming me, burning through me like acid. I need her in a way that terrifies me, in a way that makes me understand why Gabe turned everything upside down when Alba went missing, why he risked everything for one woman. I need her to be mine, completely and utterly, with no escape, no way out, no possibility of leaving. I need to mark her, to claim her, making it so that every man who looks at her knows she belongs to me, that she's mine, and she's off limits.

Chapter 10

Posey

A week has passed, and somewhere in the quiet moments between sunrise and the rest of the world waking up, we've settled into something that resembles a routine. It's not a life, not yet, but it's something. Catcher has been coming home early, earlier than I expect him to, and most nights he's been in the kitchen when I come down from my room. Some nights he's already made dinner, and he calls me down to eat with him, his voice carrying through the house with a command that's softened just enough to be almost gentle. Other nights we make it together, a strange, domestic dance of two people learning how to exist in the same space without tension crackling between them like electricity.

He takes one day off a week, always the day after a big fight, and he spends it training. Today is that day.

I wake up and make my way downstairs, my body moving through the familiar motions of the morning. The house is quiet, peaceful in a way that still surprises me. I head to the kitchen to make my oats and tea, the routine as familiar now as breathing. As I round the corner, I stop.

Catcher is at the table, a steaming cup of coffee in front of him, an ice pack held against his face. His black eyes are the first thing I notice, both of them, dark and swollen; the skin around them already turning a deep purple and blue. His eyebrow is split again, held together with what looks like surgical glue, and his bottom lip is split and swollen, the skin pulled tight and angry looking. Along is jawline, the bruising extensive and brutal. He looks like he's been through a war, and judging by the state of his face, it was vicious.

But it's not just his face that captures my attention. He's only wearing plain black shorts, no top, and his body is absolutely beautiful. His chest is a canvas of intricate tattoos, each one telling a story I don't yet know. The ink swirls across his pectoral muscles, down his ribs, covering every inch of his torso. His shoulders are broad and power- ful, the muscles defined and strong. His abdomen is carved out of muscle, each ridge visible beneath the skin is a testament to his discipline and the violence of his lifestyle. The tattoos continue down his arms, wrapping around his biceps and forearms, creating a full-body masterpiece of dark ink and powerful muscle.

I sit down at the table, trying to compose myself, trying not to stare at the sheer physicality of him. The ice pack drips slightly onto the table, and he adjusts it with a wince. I want to ask if he's okay, if he needs medical attention. Instead, I hear myself say, "Good fight then?"

His black eyes bore into mine, and even swollen and bruised, they're intense, focused entirely on me. "It was actually," he says, his voice slightly slurred from the swelling in his lip. "I haven't been up against someone really worth fighting for a while; so, it was nice."

I purse my lips at that, at the casual way he talks about destroying another human being, and I get up to make my oats and tea. I work in silence, the only sounds the soft clink of the kettle, the hum of the microwave, the gentle splash of hot water over my tea bag. I don't ask him anything else. I don't offer sympathy or concern. I just sit at the table and eat my oats, sipping my tea, watching him watch me over the rim of his coffee cup.

Even bruised and swollen, he is stunning. The Grim Reaper still looks like he walked off a GQ magazine, all dark intensity and dangerous beauty. Even after another week here, I still want to trace my fingers along his jaw, to know the weight of him on top of me, and to feel those powerful hands on my body. The thought makes heat rise in my cheeks, and I focus intently on my oats, trying to ignore the way my body responds to his presence.

Once finished, I get up and rinse my bowl, before heading upstairs to change into my training clothes. I pull on the sports bra and leggings Alba picked out for me, the fabric soft and supportive. I tie my hair back in a tight braid and head back downstairs, ready to lose myself in the familiar rhythm of training.

But as I step out onto the porch, I notice him following me. Catcher, with his battered face and ice pack, is trailing behind me like a shadow. I stop and turn to look at him, confused. He's supposed to be resting and icing his injuries, not standing in the Australian heat watching me train.

"What are you doing?" I ask, my voice cautious.

"Watching," he says simply, settling himself into one of the chairs with a slight wince. "Train."

I frown at him, uncertain, but I move to the punching bag anyway. I begin my warm-up, stretching my muscles, rolling my shoulders, preparing my body for the work ahead. I start with some light jabs, getting a feel for the bag, letting my body settle into the rhythm.

"Tighten your stance," he calls out, his voice rough from the swelling. "You're leaning too far forward."

I adjust my feet, widening my stance, grounding myself more firmly. He's right. I can feel the difference immediately, the way my power flows more efficiently through my body.

I continue, moving through my combinations, my punches and kicks becoming sharper, faster, more controlled. And he watches, offering advice as I go, his voice a steady stream of guidance and correction.

"Rotate your hips more on that kick," he instructs. "You're all arm. Use your whole body."

I adjust, feeling the difference, the power that comes from using my entire frame instead of just my limbs.

"Good," he says, and the single word sending a flutter of something through my chest. "Now faster. Don't lose the form but speed it up."

I push myself harder, my breath coming in sharp gasps, my muscles burning with exertion. And through it all, he watches, his battered face intense and focused, offering guidance and praise in equal measure. And I listen. I listen to every word, every correction, every piece of advice. Because somewhere in the last week, he's become someone whose opinion matters to me, someone whose approval I crave, someone I trust to make me better.

After about an hour, I'm exhausted, my body slick with sweat, my muscles trembling with fatigue. I step back from the bag and trying to catch my breath, trying to slow my racing heart.

"Would you like to fight?" he asks, his voice casual despite the intensity in his eyes.

I pause, my breath catching in my throat. "You would let me?" I ask, unable to keep the surprise from my voice.

He frowns, and I can see the movement causes him pain. "It's not up to me," he says, his voice firm.

I cross my arms, challenging him. "Yes, it is. You're my jailer."

"I'm not your jailer," he says again, his voice low and dangerous. "You wanna go somewhere, I'll take you. No questions asked."

I wonder if he's being genuine, if this is test or trap. But something in his voice, something in the way he's looking at me, tells me he means it. So, I decide to test it.

"I wanna go to the shops," I say, my voice steady. "I need bathroom products."

He nods, as if he's already considered this, and he's been waiting for me to ask. "Okay, we can go today. There's a Woolworths just down the road."

I stare at him, trying to gauge whether he's serious. But his expression doesn't change, his eyes don't waver. He means it.

"Okay, thank you," I say, still uncertain, still testing the boundaries of this strange freedom he's offering.

Then I ask the question that's been burning in my mind since the moment he asked. "So, I can fight if I want to?"

He shifts in his chair, and I can see him wincing at the movement. "Sure," he says. "There's heaps of leagues you can join. I can talk to a few trainers I know and see when the next women's events are coming up. It won't be underground, I'll never let you step foot in there, but you can join the baby leagues till you're ready for the bigger ones."

The offer hangs in the air between us, and I realise that this is more than just permission. This is him giving me a piece of myself back. This is him acknowledging that I'm a fighter, that I have the strength and the skill to compete, that I deserve the chance to test myself against other women. It's a gift, a freedom that comes with boundaries, but it's a gift, nonetheless.

"Okay, I'll go and shower and change, and we can go to... what did you call it? Woolworths?" I say, already moving toward the house.

He smiles, and it's a real smile, not the predatory grin I'm used to seeing. "Yes, Woolworths," he confirms.

I nod and head off the porch and up to my room. I grab the cute little blue dress I've been saving, the one that makes me feel feminine and strong at the same time. The fabric is soft and flows around my body in a way that's both modest and flattering. I head into the shower, letting the hot water cascade over my exhausted muscles, washing away the sweat and the exertion of training.

As I stand under the spray, my mind is already spinning with possibilities. I wonder if I can push him a little more, test the boundaries of his generosity. What if I asked for more than just basic bathroom products? What if I asked for good shampoo and conditioner, the kind that actually makes your hair feel soft and silky? What about a shaver, so I don't have to use the cheap disposable one I've been using? A hair dryer would be amazing, something to help style my hair instead of just letting it air dry. And makeup... God, I haven't worn makeup since before my father sold me. I would love to have some mascara, some lipstick, some foundation to even out my skin tone.

The thought actually makes me smile. Fuck. When did I start smiling about these things? When did the idea of having nice bathroom products and makeup become something that could make me happy? But it does. It makes me feel like I'm reclaiming a part of myself, the part that cares about how she looks, the part that wants to feel pretty and put together.

I finish my shower and step out, wrapping myself in a soft towel. The fabric is plush against my damp skin, and I take a moment to appreciate the simple luxury of it. I dry off slowly and deliberately, before slipping into the blue dress, letting the fabric settle against my skin. The material is cool and smooth, and it falls perfectly against my body, highlighting my curves while still maintaining an air of elegance.

I look at myself in the mirror and barely recognise the woman staring back at me. She looks healthier than she did weeks ago. Her skin has a glow from being in the sun, a golden warmth that speaks of time spent outdoors. Her muscles are more defined from all the training; more visible in her shoulders and arms. Her eyes are brighter, less haunted, filled with a spark of hope and possibility. She looks like someone who's starting to live again, not just survive.

Chapter 11

Catcher

After Posey heads upstairs to shower, I make my way to my own bathroom. My body aches in that satisfying way that comes after a brutal fight, every muscle reminds me of the violence I inflicted, of the power I wielded. I strip out of my shorts and step under the spray of hot water, letting it cascade over my bruised and battered body. The water stings against my cuts and scrapes, but it's a good pain, a pain that quiets the demons in my mind.

When I get out, I wrap a towel around my waist and head to my room to get dressed. I pull on a pair of dark blue slacks and reach for a crisp white button-up shirt. As I start to button it up, I notice my middle finger is sore, throbbing with a dull ache that shoots up my hand when I try to move it. It might be broken. I'm not entirely sure. I can still move it with almost full motion, so maybe not, but the pain suggests otherwise. I try again to do up the button on my sleeve, but the soreness makes it difficult, makes me clumsy. After a few attempts, I give up and instead roll the sleeve up to my elbow, then do the same with the other side, my sleeves never stay down long away, it's to hot this time of the year.

I grab my wallet and keys from the dresser, then shove a handgun into the back of my pants. I never go anywhere without it, never take the risk of being unprepared. I shouldn't really put it there, but it's too hot to wear the holster that goes under my jacket, and this is the only other place it isn't to notable.

I head downstairs to meet Posey, and the moment I see her everything else fades away. She's wearing a blue dress, one that makes her look both elegant and dangerous, and she's absolutely stunning. Her hair is still slightly damp from the shower, falling in waves down her back, and her skin has that fresh, clean glow that comes from just stepping out of water. She looks like she's ready to take on the world, and I want to be the man standing beside her when she does.

God, watching her train has become my new favourite hobby. The way her body moves, the strength in every punch and kick, the focus in her eyes as she works through her combinations. I let her go after training earlier, and I sat there for a few moments willing my dick to deflate and trying to regain some semblance of control. She's strong, it's clear she's been trained since she was young, and she will dominate in a real fight. I wonder if she'll take me up on the offer to join a league. I would love to see her in a real fight, circling in a ring, her body glistening with sweat as she takes down her opponent. Fuck, my dick is getting hard again just thinking about it. I adjust myself and give up on trying to control my body's response to her. Some battles aren't worth fighting.

We walk out to my SUV, and I unlock it. Opening the passenger door for her, she climbs in, I close the door before I round the vehicle and slide behind the wheel. I start the car and drive to the gate, rolling down my window to punch in the code to let us out. The gate slides open smoothly, and I drive through, heading toward Woolworths.

It's only a 20-minute drive to the nearest town with a smallish shopping centre; nothing fancy but has everything you need for the basic necessities. I find a car park and tell her to wait while I head around to open the door for her. She raises an eyebrow but doesn't say anything, just waits for me to help her out of the vehicle.

We walk into the plaza and straight into Woolworths. I grab a trolley and start pushing it as I say, "Grab anything you want, doesn't have to just be bathroom supplies."

As I make the comment, I realise something crucial. She could run right now. She could make a scene, call for help, scream for the police. But she doesn't. She just walks next to me like we're husband and wife, like this is normal, like this is what we do. and I realise, I want that. I want this domestic thing we're doing to be real. I want to walk through shops with her, buy her things, provide for her, protect her. I want a life with her, a real life, not just the captivity and control I've imposed on her.

People stare at me as we walk through the aisles, the bruises on my face standing out starkly against the crispness of my clothes. But I just stare back until they get uncomfortable and look away.

We walk through some of the aisles; only stopping in the ones she wants. I watch as she browses the hair products and other items, placing things carefully in the trolley. She doesn't stop, just keeps adding items, and I realise I would buy the whole damn place if it made her smile. I've never had a girlfriend or anything before, never had anyone to care for in this way, and half the things she puts in the cart I didn't even know she needed. I provided basic needs, shampoo, soap, toothpaste, but she's getting hair masks and some fancy pink razor and so many other things I hadn't even realised she needed. And I feel bad. I feel like I haven't really been looking after her, like I've just given her basic necessities without considering what would make her feel cared for, what would make her feel like a woman, instead of just a captive.

When she finally dusts her hands off and says, "I really wanted a hair dryer, but they don't seem to sell those here," I smile and say, "There's a chemist out there. They might have one. We can check. It's one of those big warehouse style ones."

She nods and says, "Okay."

We head to the till and ring everything up. The total is substantial, but I don't even glance at it. I just pull out my wallet and pay, watching as she doesn't say a word, doesn't thank me, doesn't acknowledge the amount. She just accepts it, accepts my care, accepts that I want to provide for her. And that's enough. That's more than enough.

I push the trolley out and lead her to the chemist, it's a large warehouse style store with rows and rows of products. She walks the aisles again, carefully selecting items and placing them in the cart. More hair products, skincare items, and then makeup. Not a lot, but it's there, some mascara, lipstick, foundation. She picks up some perfume and tests it on her wrist, sniffing it thoughtfully before moving on, to the next one till she finds one she likes.

Then she turns to me and asks, "What cologne do you wear?"

I smile at her, pleased that she's asking, pleased that she cares enough to want to know. "Tom Ford, Oud Wood," I say. "Why?"

"It smells amazing on your skin," she says, and the compliment hits me harder than any punch ever could. It's simple, straightforward, but it means something coming from her.

She starts looking at the men's colognes, walking slowly down the aisle, examining each bottle with careful attention. I watch her, realising something crucial. Women love to shop, love to touch things, to explore, to choose. It makes me wonder if her father ever let her shop like this, or if this is in fact the first time she's been allowed to just grab what she wants without permission, without fear of punishment. The thought makes my jaw clench with rage at the man who sold her, who controlled her, who never gave her these simple freedoms that most people take for granted.

She picks up a few different colognes and smells them, turning her nose up at some, her expression thoughtful and discerning. Then she grabs another one, sniffs it, and tilts her head, considering it. She walks over to me and says, "Hold out your hand."

I do, and she sprays the cologne on my wrist, the scent immediately filling the space between us. It's warm and spicy, with notes of amber and sandalwood, and it smells fucking incredible. Better than incredible. She places the bottle back on the shelf and then comes back to me, leaning in close to smell my arm. Her proximity makes my heart race, makes my dick harden in my slacks, makes me want to pull her against me and never let go.

She smiles, and it's a real smile, genuine and warm, and she says, "I like this one. Can I grab it?"

I raise my eyebrows and ask, "For me?"

"Well yes, who else?" she says with a hint of amusement in her voice. "You're not caging more people in your house, are you?"

I shake my head with a smirk, and she says, "Of course you, then."

"Okay," I say, and she places the bottle in the cart with all the other things she's selected, her choices a reflection of who she is and what she wants.

We head to the till, where again everything is rung up and she stands and waits for me, just looking around, cataloguing her surroundings like she always does. I pay without hesitation, without even looking at the total. Money means nothing to me. Hasn't my whole life, that's what happens when you have always had an abundance for it, I've never known a world where I had to count my penny's or check my account. Last time I checked my account was when I bought an apartment in the city, and I think that was two years ago, and I only checked it because I wanted to pay for the apartment with cash, so I needed to log on for the accountant to have the money ready for the sale.

We leave the chemist, and I stop at the trolley return by

the entrance. I grab all the bags in one hand, my maybe broken finger protesting at holding the bags and then reach out with my other hand for her. I watch as her mind plays around with the idea of holding my hand for a bit, and I can see the internal conflict playing out across her face. The hesitation, the desire, the fear. But then she reaches out and takes my hand, and we walk back to the car hand in hand.

Fucking hell, I love it. I love the idea of her, love the way her hand feels in mine, love the fact that she chose to hold my hand without being forced. Her hand is warm and so much smaller than mine, fitting perfectly in my palm. I want her to slide right into my side, to feel the heat of her body against mine; I want to make it hard for me to walk, just so I can keep her close.

Chapter 12

Posey

When we get home, Catcher carries all my shopping bags up to my room without being asked, without me having to say a word. He sets them down on my bed and starts helping me unpack, his large hands carefully removing each item and setting it aside so I can organise it. It's such a simple thing, such a domestic gesture, and it twists something deep inside me. My father never helped me with anything. He ordered me around, controlled every aspect of my life, but he never helped. He never cared enough to do something so small and so significant.

I watch as Catcher unpacks the hair products, the makeup, the perfume, the razor. He handles each item with care, like it matters to him that I have these things, like my happiness is important. And I don't know how to reconcile that with the man who stole me from being trafficked. Maybe the main thing I should really be focusing on is this: this man took me from a fate much, much worse than this, and given me freedom, albeit caged. And he hasn't asked me for anything in return. He's given me choice, agency, respect.

As we unpack, he moves closer to me, and I find myself backed into the corner of the room, surrounded by his presence. He's so large, so imposing, but there's nothing threatening about it. Instead, it feels safe. It feels like being protected by something powerful and dangerous that has chosen to be gentle with me. He reaches up and brushes a strand of hair off my face, his fingers gentle against my skin. The touch sends a jolt of electricity through me, and I find myself holding my breath, afraid that if I move, this moment will shatter.

My own hand comes up almost of its own accord, my fingers tracing the bruises on his face. His jaw is still swollen and discoloured, the skin around his eyes a deep purple and blue. I can see the pain he's been in, the pain he's endured, and I want to soothe it away, want to make it better. I want to kiss each bruise and make the hurt disappear.

"Does your face still hurt?" I ask, my voice barely above a whisper.

"No," he says, and I know he's lying. I can see it in the way he winces when he moves, in the careful way he doesn't open his mouth too much to talk. But he's lying for me, trying to make me feel better, trying to protect me from worrying about him.

I start to pull my hand away, but he moves it back, pressing my palm against his cheek. "Don't stop," he says, his voice low and rough, almost pleading.

I gulp, my heart racing in my chest like a wild bird

trapped in a cage. The moment feels suspended in time, like the entire world has stopped spinning just for us, like we're the only two people that matter. "Are you going to kiss me?" I ask, the question tumbling out before I can stop it, before I can think about the consequences.

He leans back just slightly, his dark eyes search mine, searching for doubt or fear or hesitation. "Only if you want me to," he says, giving me the choice, giving me the agency that I've been denied for so long. He's asking permission, treating me like my desires matter, like I matter.

And I do. God, I really, really do. I want to know what his lips taste like, want to feel the weight of him against me, want to surrender to this thing that's been building between us. I want him in a way that terrifies but exhilarates me at the same time.

"Yes," I whisper, the word barely audible but enough.

He leans in slowly, giving me time to change my mind, giving me time to pull away. But I don't. I stay exactly where I am, my hand still on his cheek, my eyes locked on his. And then his lips meet mine.

It's soft at first, tentative, like he's afraid he'll break me if he pushes too hard. But I don't want soft. I want the intensity that I've seen in him, the passion that he keeps locked away behind those dark eyes. I press into him, my free hand coming up to grip his shirt, and he responds immediately. His hand comes up cupping the back of my head, his fingers threading through my hair, and he deepens the kiss.

It's everything I imagined and nothing like I expected. His lips are firm and warm, and he tastes like coffee and something uniquely him. The kiss is possessive and tender at the same time; a contradiction that somehow makes perfect sense. He's claiming me, marking me as his, but he's also asking, checking in to make sure I'm okay with this.

He pulls me against him tightly, his body pressing mine further into the corner, causing me to moan into the kiss. His body is all hard ridges and lines, every muscle defined and powerful beneath the fabric of his shirt; I want to explore every inch of him. I can taste copper suddenly, and I realise his lip must have opened again from the kiss. I pull back slightly, reacting to it immediately,

"Shit, I'm sorry," I begin, my concern overriding everything else.

He smirks, and despite the blood on his lip, he looks absolutely wicked; like an angel before they fall, who's just discovered sin. "Why did you stop?" he asks, his voice low and rough, almost accusatory.

"You're bleeding!" I say, like it's a shock, like he had no idea he has reopened his lip during the kiss.

He growls, a sound that reverberating through his chest and into mine, a sound that makes my entire body respond. "A little blood will not kill me," he says, his eyes dark with desire and intensity. "And I was just getting to find out how good you taste, Posey. I'll stop if you want me to. But just know, I don't want to."

My eyes dart from one of his to the next, searching for the truth in his gaze. I want more. I want all of him. But he's hurt, and I'm worried about making it worse. Do I stop? Do I pull away and be the responsible one? Do I protect him from himself?

As if reading my mind, he leans in close and whispers against my lips, "If you think a few bruises are going to stop me from claiming you, you would be wrong, Posey."

Fuck it.

I lean back in, our lips crashing with renewed intensity. Hitting him with all the passion and desire I've been holding back. And he responds immediately, his hands gripping my waist, his fingers digging in just enough to leave marks, to claim me. He lifts me effortlessly, carrying me over to my bed. He lays me out on it, and I feel the shopping bags beneath me, the items I bought earlier now scattered across the mattress.

"Shit," I mutter, suddenly aware of the mess, suddenly aware that this is happening, that we're actually doing this.

"Nope," he says, already moving, already making a decision. "My bed is empty."

He picks me back up, my legs wrapping around his waist automatically, and walks me down to his room. Our eyes are locked on each other the entire way, and I feel like I'm falling, like I'm surrendering completely to whatever this is between us. There's no going back from this moment. Everything changes now.

He walks me into his room and stops at the end of his bed. He lowers me back to the floor gently, his hands lingering on my waist for just a moment longer than necessary. Then he takes a step back from me, creating distance, creating space for what's about to happen. His eyes are dark with desire, his breathing ragged and his chest heaving with barely controlled need, as he pulls a gun from the back of his pants and lays it on the chest of draws behind him.

"Have you been wondering how heavy I would be on your tongue?" he asks, his voice dripping with filth and desire. "How far I could cram my dick down your throat, Posey?"

My pussy clenches on nothing at his words because he isn't wrong. I have been thinking exactly that. I've been fantasising about this moment for a while now, imagining what it would feel like to have him like this, to have him at my mercy. The thought is intoxicating.

I lower myself to the floor in front of him, sinking to my knees deliberately slow. The carpet is soft beneath me, and I feel the weight of what I'm about to do settle over me. This is power. This is control. This is me choosing him, choosing this.

He curses out loud at the sight of me down there, his voice strained and raw. "You look so pretty for me on your knees, Posey," he says, his voice rough and strained. "Pull my dick out."

My hands reach for him, my fingers working quickly to undo his belt, then his slacks. I lower the zipper slowly, my eyes never leaving his. The anticipation is almost unbearable, a tension that builds with each passing second. I pull his slacks down, before I arch back up to grab the waistband of his boxers. His hard dick springs free, and I have to catch my breath.

He isn't massive at all, but his dick is thick. The girth on this man would stretch me so good, would fill me completely to the point I would feel every inch of him. I lean in and lick the pre-cum off the tip of his dick, and he moans at the contact, a sound that's almost pained.

"Oh, little bird," he says, his voice filled with praise and desire. "You spoil me."

I do it again and again, licking the pre-cum away, tasting him, savouring the salt of his skin. Then I lick from the base to the tip, deliberately taking my time, savouring every moment. All the while, he praises me for doing a good job, his words of encouragement spurring me on, making me want to please him more.

I can feel his legs locking, his muscles tensing beneath my hands as I reach out with my other hand to cup his balls. They tighten and draw up, and I know he's close. His praises have become random words, just spoken aloud, fragmented and desperate. Bringing a man to this point is the most empowering feeling I've ever experienced. It makes a man so filled with lust he can't talk more than a few curse words and your name. It's intoxicating, knowing that I have this power over him, knowing that I can bring the Grim Reaper to his knees, knowing that I can bring this dangerously violent man completely undone, by simply licking his dick.

I want to taste his cum. I want to feel him come apart because of me. I wrap my whole mouth around his dick and suck hard, my other hand squeezing his balls. He nearly crashes to his knees as he explodes in my mouth, his hot cum filling me, landing on my tongue. The salty taste of him lingers, coating my mouth, and I continue to suck until he stops, until his body stops shaking with the force of his orgasm. He manages to straighten his legs again, his breathing ragged and harsh as his entire body trembles.

I lean back and look up at him, my eyes searching his,

suddenly uncertain; suddenly needing his approval, "Did I do it right?" I ask, my voice small and vulnerable.

The look he gives me could stop wars in their tracks. He looks like I just handed him the world, like I've given him something more precious than anything else could ever be.

Chapter 13

Catcher

I stand there staring down at Posey, my mind completely blank except for one thought: holy fucking shit.

I just came from being licked. That's all she did, just licked me, took me into her mouth, and it felt like she had sucked the soul from my body. I've had women before, plenty of them, but nothing, absolutely nothing, has ever felt like this. It's like she reached inside me and pulled something out, something essential, something I didn't even know I had to give.

My mother was right. She was right all those years ago when she told me that one day I would come across a woman who would change the course of my life. And that woman is on her knees in front of me, looking up at me with those brown eyes, asking if she did it right. She did more than right. She did everything. She is everything.

I want to hand her the world right now. I want to give her everything she's ever wanted, everything she's ever dreamed of. I want to make sure that she never wants for anything, that she never has to ask for anything, that she knows without a shadow of a doubt that I would give her anything she asks for. Anything. Everything. My entire world.

My hand reaches out to brush her cheek, my fingers gentle against her skin. "You, my little bird, did better than okay," I say, my voice rough, strained with the weight of what I'm feeling. "Now let me show you just how much I appreciate it."

I hold my hand out for her to take, and she does, her small hand fitting perfectly in mine. I help her stand, pulling her up slowly, my eyes never leaving hers. I lean straight in and kiss her deeply with all the intensity and passion of what I'm feeling; all the possession, the need and something that feels dangerously close to love.

The blood from my lip mixes with the taste of her and me, and it's the most erotic thing I've ever experienced. There's something perfect about it, something raw and honest and real. She tastes like me, like my cum; the only evidence of what she just did to me. And I want to taste her like this forever. There will never be a day where this isn't enough. There will never be a day where I don't want her like this.

She melts into me, completely melts, her body going soft and pliant against mine. The feeling of a woman just melting, completely intoxicated by me, is a desire I never knew I had wanted to experience. The women I've fucked in the past were always a little shy or scared of me, probably because of my size, and what I do for a living. But Posey just melts, like she knows I won't hurt her, like she trusts me completely. It's a power trip unlike anything I've ever experienced, and it makes me want to protect her with every fibre of my being.

I deepen the kiss, my hands coming up to grip her waist, pulling her closer, needing to feel every inch of her against me. She responds immediately, her hands coming up to grip my shirt, her body pressing into mine. I can feel her heartbeat against my chest, racing just as fast as mine, and I know that she's feeling this too; this moment means as much to her as it means to me.

I pull back just enough to say to her, my voice low and commanding. "Pull that dress off, Posey. I want to see you naked."

She does, stepping from my grip and slowly pulling that cute as fuck dress she wore over her head, leaving her in a small white underset. She slowly slips from that too, and I watch as her breasts tumble free. They're not big, not by conventional standards, all that training and fighting she's done over the years has robbed her of ever having large breasts, but what is there is absolutely stunning. They're like little ski slopes, fuller at the bottom than the top, creating the best under boob I've ever seen. Her waist is thin, and a slight six-pack is showing as she moves, leading down to slightly wide hips and thick, thick thighs that look like they could crush a man between them. And between her thighs is a small patch of hair, not a lot, she's kept it trimmed, but a small patch that points to the exact spot I want to bury my face. It's like a little sign that says everything you've dreamed of for weeks lies here.

I take a moment to just look at her, to appreciate the strength and beauty of her, to realise that this incredible woman is mine. She's standing before me completely vulnerable, completely exposed, and she trusts me. The weight of that trust settles over me like a mantle.

"Crawl back onto the bed, Posey," I say, my voice rough with need. "On your back."

She does, crawling on her hands and knees up the bed, her body moving with a grace and power that makes my dick harden all over again. She settles back on my pillows, her brown hair spread out there like silk, and I hope her scent is clinging to my sheets, clinging to everything in this room. I want to smell her everywhere, want to be surrounded by her even when she's not here.

"Now spread those thighs," I command, my voice low and dangerous. "I wanna see what's mine."

She spreads them wide, showing me her pretty pink pussy, and I nearly lose my mind. She's wet and ready, her arousal evident, and I know she wants me as much as I want her. I quickly unbutton my shirt and let it fall off, then I toe my shoes off and step fully from my pants and boxers. I crawl up the bed, settling between her thighs. My nose burying itself there, and I take a deep lung full of her arousal, breathing her in like she's the only oxygen I need to survive.

"Fuck," I growl, the word torn from deep in my chest.

Using one hand, I part her pussy lips, and I can see how slick she is, how wet and ready to take me. I know she wants me; it's dripping from her entrance. My tongue darts out and licks it up, her taste exploding on my tongue like nothing I've ever experienced. It's sweet and salty and just her, and I'm immediately addicted. I want to spend the rest of my life tasting her like this.

"Fuck me," I say, then dive in and eat.

I eat her pussy like a man starved, like she's a drink of water in the desert and I'm dying of thirst. My hands grip her tight on either side of her thighs as I pull her pussy as tightly into my face as I can, needing to taste every inch of her, needing to make her feel as good as she made me feel. She is moaning and writhing on the bed, panting as I keep licking and sucking on her clit, my tongue working her over with single-minded focus.

"Oh, Catcher," she moans, her hips bucking up against my face, and I grip her tighter, holding her in place so I can continue my assault on her senses.

I can feel her getting closer, can feel the way her thighs are starting to tremble, the way her breathing is becoming more ragged. I want to push her over the edge, want to make her come on my tongue, want to taste her orgasm. I increase my pace, my tongue flicking over her clit faster and faster, and then she's coming, her body going rigid as waves of pleasure wash over her.

"Catcher!" she screams, my name like a prayer on her lips. I continue to lick her through her orgasm, savouring every moment, every sound, every tremor of her body.

When she finally comes down from her high, I pull back and look up at her, my face glistening with her arousal. "That's one," I say, my voice rough with satisfaction and promise.

Then I let her thighs go and slap her pussy hard with my hand. The sound is wet and obscene, and she moans at the contact. I do it again, and again, until her pussy lips are all swollen and ready for more. I rub her clit with my finger, but I wince, fuck, that's the one that hurts from the fight. I switch back to the hand I used to slap her with and circle her clit. I move down to her pussy's entrance, slowly slipping in two fingers.

I watch as her pussy swallows them, gripping them tightly, and I ask, "Do you think you can take three, Posey? I need you a lot wider than this for me."

I pull out and push three in. It's tight, gods so tight. Her pussy makes me go slow, pulling in and out at small intervals over and over until I manage to get them all the way in. She moans every time I bottom out, her body responding to every movement. I curl them and use the come-hither motion, and she squirms a little more, her hips bucking against my hand.

Then I lower my face back down to her pussy and lick her clit over and over, my tongue working her relentlessly. I can feel her pussy getting tighter, getting closer to another orgasm. I lean back up quickly, I don't want to miss it, and settle myself between her thighs, my dick as dark as steel now, pre-cum dripping from the tip. It wants to be inside her cunt now, but it's going to have to wait a little bit longer.

I start to pump my fingers a little bit faster, but also pushing them deeper and deeper, my knuckles hitting her opening. I would love to work her up to take my whole fist, fuck, seeing my hand disappear inside her would have me coming without needing to touch her, but not today. Not yet. We have time. All the time in the world.

I look at Posey's face as she looks down and watches me fill her pussy with my fingers. "Do you wanna know what it's like to take my cock, Posey?" I ask, my voice low and intense.

She swallows, her eyes wide and filled with desire and anticipation. "Yes," she says, the word barely a whisper.

"Then be a good girl for me," I say, my voice dropping to a growl. "And cum."

I finger her hard and fast, my movements becoming more aggressive, more demanding. Her pussy strangles my fingers and her orgasm starts. The second I feel her clamp down I pull my fingers free and shove my dick to her opening and push. I push and push, stretching her pussy wide while she comes apart, while her body convulses around me. Then I pump hard and fast, grabbing her hips as her orgasm continues to roll through her.

Her pussy is so tight on me, it's a struggle to pull out and push in. My girth is big, I know this, but there's something magical about pushing in while a woman is convulsing on you. I shove myself balls deep, rubbing her clit with my finger as I continue to pull in and out. She's whimpering now, her pussy going slack as she says, "Stop, I'm too sensitive."

But I don't stop. Fuck no, this is my thing. This is what I love. One hand grips her hip, and I pound hard and deep, my balls slapping her body as I continue, my other hand rubs her clit over and over. Her eyes are wide, and I see the shock on her face as another orgasm rips through her out of nowhere. Her back arches, her eyes rolling back, and I explode. I fill her up with my cum, making sure every single drop is deep inside her pussy, marking her as mine from the inside out.

I still and look down at her. She's panting hard, her eyes now closed, her pussy pulsing on my dick, sweat on her forehead and body. I lean down over the top of her, my lips finding hers as I place gentle kisses there, over and over again. "You did so well, little bird," I say against her lips, my voice tender and full of praise. "You're such a good girl. You took me like you were made for me."

And right now, I know with absolute certainty that she was. She was made for me. There's no one else in this world who can ever compare to her, no one else who can ever make me feel this way. She's mine, completely and utterly mine. Even if that means I have to keep her caged.

Chapter 14

Posey

I sit out in the hot sun, letting it warm my skin; it's slowly becoming my favourite place here. The past week has flown by, a little bit like Groundhog Day, but in the best possible way. Every night, I sleep in Catcher's bed because he demands it. If I try to sleep in mine, I wake up to him carrying me to his bed, telling me to stay in his, please. There's something tender about it, the way he insists on having me close to him while he sleeps. It makes me feel wanted, needed, important.

He's been working late every day, but he tells me what he's been doing. Last night, he got home at 2 AM because they turned up to one of the brothels they were going to take over and found it guarded. They, of course, took them out; I don't ask for details, and I don't want to know the specifics of the violence, but Catcher had to wait for the clean-up crew. The reality of what he does, the darkness of his world, should scare me. And sometimes it does. But mostly, I'm just grateful that he's using his power and his position to dismantle the very system that was going to destroy me.

He has a fight tonight, so he's home until then. He needs to train, and he's been helping me train first thing, every morning. And I'm shocked with how much I've progressed. I was good before, but now I really feel the power behind my kicks, the strength in my punches. He's been coaching me, correcting my form, pushing me harder, and it's made all the difference.

I watch him through the glass windows as he moves around the kitchen, making us lunch. He's shirtless again, his tattooed body on full display, and I can't help but admire him. The bruises from his last fight are gone, but I know that by the end of tonight, after he steps out of the ring again, he'll have collected new ones. The thought makes my stomach twist with worry, which is a little annoying. I never meant to care about my captor.

He catches me watching him and smirks, a dangerous smirk that makes my heart race. He knows I'm watching. He always knows. He winks at me through the glass, and I feel heat rise in my cheeks. Even after a week of sleeping in his bed, of him touching me in all the right places, he still makes me blush.

I stand up and head inside, the cool air of the house a shock after the heat outside. He's setting out sandwiches on the counter, and I move to help him, but he pulls me against him, wrapping his arms around me from behind.

"How are you feeling about tonight?" I ask, my voice soft.

"Good," he says, his lips finding a sensitive spot on my

neck. "I'm ready to fight. But I'm also ready to come home to you."

The words make my heart skip a beat. He's been saying things like this all week, things that make it clear that I'm not just a captive anymore, that I'm something more to him. And I'm not sure how I feel about it.

I turn in his arms and lean all the way up, kissing him passionately, pouring all my need and desire into the kiss. When I pull back, I'm breathless and flushed, and I can see the desire in his eyes.

"Can I come and watch?" I ask softly, my voice barely above a whisper. "I want to go with you. I want to see you fight."

He stiffens, his hands tightening on my waist. "No," he says immediately, his voice firm and final.

"Please," I say again, knowing I'm manipulating him, knowing I'm using the kiss and my body to get what I want. But I do want this. I hate being locked up here all the time. It's been a whole week since he took me to Woolworths, and being stuck at home, even in this beautiful house, is suffocating. "I hate being locked up here all the time. You'll be there. I'll be safe, right?"

He takes a deep breath, his jaw clenching as he processes my request. I can see the internal struggle playing out across his face, the conflict between his desire to keep me safe and his understanding that I need more freedom.

"I don't know if you can see that," he says carefully, his voice strained.

"See what?" I ask, though I know exactly what he means.

"Someone die? Because I've seen that before, Catcher. I grew up in France with a crime boss father. I've seen death. I've seen violence. I'm not naive about what you do."

The memory flashes through my mind before I can stop it. I was ten years old, looking for my father in his office. One of his lackeys had been skimming from the drug supply, and my father had found out. I walked in to find my father standing over the man with a gun pressed to his head. I remember the fear in the man's eyes, the way he was begging, pleading for his life. His voice was shaking, desperate, and I could see the sweat on his forehead. And then the gun fired. The sound of it still echoes in my head sometimes, late at night when I can't sleep. It was so loud, so final, so absolute.

I had been shaken up for weeks after that. I couldn't eat, couldn't sleep, couldn't stop seeing that man's face. I kept having nightmares where I was the one with the gun to my head, my father was pointing it at me. But eventually, I grew numb to it. My father's world was one of violence and death, and if I wanted to survive in it, I had to learn to accept that. I had to learn to be strong. I had to learn not to flinch. I had to learn that death was just another part of life in this world.

So, I've seen death. I've seen what violence looks like up close; and yes, it scares me to think about Catcher killing someone. But it doesn't shock me. It doesn't make me think less of him. It just makes me understand him better. It makes me realise that we're not so different, he and I. We're both products of a violent world, both shaped by darkness and danger.

He growls, a sound that reverberates through his chest

and into mine. "Well, I would like it if you didn't see me kill someone," he says, his voice rough and strained, almost vulnerable. The admission that he doesn't want me to see that side of him, the killer side, touches something deep inside me.

I reach up and cup his face in my hands, forcing him to look at me. My thumbs trace his cheekbones, and I can feel the tension in his jaw beneath my palms, his eyes draw me in every time I look into them, they are so dark, like a demon has taken over and lives inside them, but there is so much depth in there, if only one would take a few minutes to really look.

"How about I watch you fight and close my eyes when it's at the end?" I ask, my voice soft and persuasive. "I want to see you at work. I want to see you fight. And I mean it, Catcher." Seeing this man, this weapon, work would be beautiful.

He stares at me for a long moment, his dark eyes searching mine, trying to determine if I'm being sincere or if I'm just manipulating him. The truth is, I'm doing both. I am manipulating him, using my body and my words to get what I want. But I also genuinely want to see him fight. I want to see this side of him, the dangerous, powerful side that makes him who he is. I want to understand him completely, to see him in his element, to witness the power and skill that makes him legendary in the underground fighting world.

"You're manipulating me," he says finally, but there's no anger in his voice, just resignation and something that might be amusement.

"Yes," I admit, not bothering to deny it. "But I also

mean every word. Please, Catcher. I need to get out of this house. I need to see you. I need to understand this part of your world."

He's quiet for a long moment, and I can see him wrestling with the decision. Finally, he sighs and says, "Fine. But you stay with Gabe the entire time. You don't leave his side. And if it gets too much, you tell him, and he gets you out of there. Understood?"

Relief floods through me, and I lean up and kiss him again, this time with genuine gratitude and affection. "Thank you," I whisper against his lips. "Thank you."

He pulls back and looks at me seriously. "I mean it, Posey. You stay close. You stay safe. And you close your eyes at the end. I don't want you seeing that."

"I will," I promise, and I mean it. "I will."

Chapter 15

Catcher

I'm packing my bag for the fight, putting in a good set of fighting shorts. If Posey is coming, I actually want to look good. I feel like an idiot for wanting to do that, but I'm also a little elated by the thought. The feelings I'm feeling isn't something I'm used to. I've never cared what I looked like for a woman before. I've never wanted to impress anyone. But Posey is different. She's changed everything.

I refuse to give her up, so I just have to get used to these feelings. I have to accept that this woman has completely upended my world and I'm okay with that.

I pull out my phone and dial Gabe's number. He picks up on the second ring.

"Yeah?" he answers, his voice distracted.

"Posey's coming tonight," I say, not bothering with preamble. I know how this is going to go.

There's a long pause. Then, "No. Absolutely not."

"Yes," I say firmly, my jaw clenching. "She's coming."

"Catcher, " Gabe starts, but I cut him off.

"I'm not leaving her at home. She's coming. Deal with it."

I can hear him take a deep breath on the other end of the line, and I can practically see him running a hand through his hair in frustration. The silence stretches between us, heavy with tension.

"You're making my life more complicated, you know that, right?" he says finally, his voice tight with exasperation.

"I know," I say, and I do know. But I'm not sorry. She asked to come, and I seem incapable of saying no to her. Gabe sighs, a long, drawn-out sound of resignation. "Fine. Okay. Fine. But I'm not telling Alba she's coming, or she'll want to come too. And I can't keep my eyes on both of them. It will send me absolutely fucking crazy."

I can't help but laugh at that. The image of Gabe trying to keep track of both Alba and Posey at the fight club is almost too much. "Okay, fair enough. I'll keep her close."

"You better," Gabe says, and then he hangs up.

I grab my bag and walk down to meet Posey in the kitchen, stopping dead in my tracks.

She's wearing tight jeans that hug her curves perfectly, and a tight long sleeve top that shows off her toned arms and the strength in her shoulders. She looks insane. Her ass is like candy in these jeans, I thought she looked good in a dress, but seeing her like this, I was wrong. This right here is the right way for her to dress. This is what makes her look a million dollars to me.

"Fuck," I breathe, unable to stop myself.

She frowns and says, "Do I need to change? I was hoping to blend in and not stand out."

"Little bird," I say, walking toward her, "you could wear a cardboard box, and you would still look like my favourite treat."

She blushes, and that little blush is my favourite thing to see. I pull her into me, and her hands grab my shirt as I lean down to her.

"You're going to distract me looking this good, you know," I say, my voice low and rough with desire.

She gulps and says, "Sorry."

"Don't say sorry," I say, then kiss her, pouring all my need and desire into the kiss.

She has a thin amount of makeup on, not a lot, but the black on her eyes makes her deep chocolate colour stand out so well. "Fuck," I breathe into the kiss, my dick getting hard in my slacks as I say, "I wanna bend you over that counter and fuck you, but we've really gotta go."

She laughs into the kiss and says, "Come on then," and grips my hard dick through my slacks, making me groan. "I'll fix this later, okay? A treat for winning."

I gulp because this woman has me by the balls, literally and figuratively, and I love it. I love her. The realisation makes me feel a little sick in the guts, and I pull back from the kiss to look at her.

"What?" she asks, her eyes searching mine.

"Nothing," I say, but it's everything. "Come on. We gotta go."

I take her hand and lead her to the car, my mind reeling with the realisation that I'm completely and utterly in love with this woman.

When we reach the SUV, I open the passenger door for her and help her inside. As she settles into the seat, I reach across and click her seatbelt in for her, even though she's perfectly capable of doing it herself. But I like doing it. I like taking care of her like this. My father used to do it for my mother, open doors, click her seatbelt, carry her bags, make food for her all the time. He treated her like she was the most precious thing in his world, and I find that I now enjoy doing the same for Posey.

I walk around to my side and get in, starting the engine. As I drive toward the gate, I notice her watching me as I punch in the code. She tries to memorise it, I can tell by the way her eyes track my fingers. I wonder if maybe she's okay with it all now, or if one day she'll ask to leave. Will I let her? No. That answer is simple. But what if she chooses to stay like Alba did? What if I can give her the code knowing she'll come back, like a half-caged bird? The idea still makes me sick, but not in a bad way. More of an, I want to keep her safe way.

The drive to the club is quiet, charged with anticipation. When we arrive, I park in my spot and turn to her.

"Now it's loud and mean in there," I say, my voice dropping to a commanding tone. "Stick to my side. Follow me. And stay where I tell you to."

She nods and leans over to kiss my lips softly. "Okay," she says, and the simple word carries so much weight.

I realise I'm nervous. Nervous at her seeing me fight, but also nervous because now she will have a target on her back. Everyone will know I have a weakness. Everyone will know that Posey is important to me, and in this world, that makes her a liability. But I can't send her home. I won't.

I get out and open her door, helping her out of the

SUV. I place an arm over her shoulders and pull her close, walking her toward the entrance. It's loud like usual, a fight is currently going on, and as I walk through the crowd, it parts for me like normal. People know who I am. They know what I'm capable of. And now they're going to see that I have something to lose.

I walk her straight to the change room, where Gabe and Aurelio are waiting. They both look up as we enter, and I can see the surprise flash across their faces when they see Posey.

Gabe steps forward first, his expression shifting to something more controlled. He holds out his hand to Posey; his movements deliberate and polite. "Gabe," he says simply. "It's nice to properly meet you."

Posey takes his hand, and I watch as they shake. Her grip is firm, confident. She doesn't flinch or look away.

"Posey," she says in return. "Thank you for letting me come."

Gabe nods, and then Aurelio steps forward. He's taller than Gabe, broader in the shoulders, with a scar that runs down the side of his face. But his expression is gentle as he holds out his hand to her.

"Aurelio," he says, his voice warm. "Welcome."

Posey shakes his hand as well, and I can see her relax slightly. These are my brothers, and they're treating her with respect. That means something.

"Sorry for the first impression," Gabe says, and there's genuine apology in his voice.

"It's okay," Posey says smoothly. "Catcher explained it to me."

Gabe looks at me and raises a brow. I know what he's

thinking. He knows that if I said anything along those lines, it must be serious. And it is.

I strip out of my clothes and pull on my fighting shorts. Aurelio is already wrapping my hands, his movements practiced and efficient. He's done this a hundred times before. Gabe rubs vaseline over my shoulders and chest, working it into my skin with firm, practiced strokes. It's a ritual we've perfected over the years.

When Aurelio finishes wrapping my hands, I hold one out toward Posey and say, "We're up in a minute. Let's go wait."

She takes my hand, and then she does something that makes my heart skip a beat. She brings my wrapped hand to her mouth and kisses it softly. I know what that means. It's a good luck kiss. It's a win the match kiss, her way of saying go out there and come back to me.

I wrap my arms around her shoulders and kiss the top of her head, breathing in the scent of her. When I pull back, I see Gabe looking at me with his eyebrows raised, a smirk playing at the corners of his mouth. Aurelio gives a whipping motion toward me, making a joke about how whipped I am. I just smirk at him because fuck it. He's right. I am whipped on her. Completely and utterly whipped.

We walk out to the ring, and I lead Posey to where we'll be sitting. Gabe has already filled the row of seats behind us with armed men, so when we sit down, I know no one can touch us from behind. It's a nice comfort, knowing she's protected from all angles.

The clean-up crew has just finished with the last fight. Someone is now drying the floor of the ring with a towel, making sure the mats are not wet from mopping up the blood from the last fight. The smell of it lingers in the air, metallic and sharp. I wonder if Posey notices it, if it makes her uncomfortable. But when I glance at her, her eyes are focused on the ring, with a hungry look on her face.

The presenter's voice booms through the warehouse. "Now we have the feature fight! Catcher, our undefeated champion, is going against Milan, who is making his debut fight. Who is gonna make it home?"

The crowd erupts in cheers and boos. Most of them are betting on me, but there are always those who want to see the champion fall. I lean over to Posey and say, "Watch me, little bird. Watch me fight for you."

Chapter 16

Posey

Catcher stands and leans down to kiss me gently, his lips soft against mine for just a moment. Then he turns and walks toward the opening of the ring. The crowd erupts in cheers and boos, a cacophony of sound that makes my heart race and my palms sweat. I watch as he walks through the opening with the grace and power of a predator, completely at ease in this environment. He belongs here. This is his world.

The next fighter walks in, and my breath catches in my throat. He's massive, like Catcher, with a shaved head and a menacing look on his face that makes my skin crawl. This is Milan, I think. The presenter called him that. He looks like he's ready to kill, and the realisation hits me hard: these fights are to the death.

I'm scared. Absolutely terrified, if I'm being honest with myself. As excited as I am to see Catcher fight, to see him in his element, I'm scared he might die. These fights have a 50/50 chance of survival. Those are not good odds. Catcher is the undefeated champ, and Gabe and Aurelio look calm, like they know he will win. I hope their calm is a good sign. I hope they know something I don't. I hope that their confidence in him is justified.

Catcher stands in the middle of the ring now, and Milan meets him there. They bump their wrapped hands together in a gesture of respect, before they spread apart. I swallow hard and keep my eyes on Catcher. His body language is completely different from Milan's. While Milan is tense and aggressive; coiled like a spring ready to explode, Catcher is loose and relaxed. He looks calm. His eyes are dark, and he doesn't even look bothered as he waits for the fight to begin. He looks like he's about to go for a walk, not step into a fight to the death.

The ref claps his hands, and they start to circle each other. The presenter is talking, his voice booming through the warehouse, but I'm not listening at all. I can't hear anything except the sound of my own heartbeat, thundering in my ears like a drum. It's so loud I'm surprised no one else can hear it.

As I watch them circle, mesmerised by Catcher's movement. He's like a dancer, fluid and precise, his footwork impeccable. Milan, on the other hand, is all brute force and aggression. He's looking for an opening, looking for a way to use his size against Catcher. He's looking for a way to end this quickly.

Then Milan lunges, a wild haymaker that would destroy anyone it connected with. But Catcher is faster. He sidesteps it with minimal movement, letting Milan's momentum carry him past. The crowd gasps, and I realise I've been holding my breath.

"Come on," I whisper, my hands clenching into fists so hard my nails dig into my palms. "Come on, Catcher."

Gabe leans over to me and says quietly, "He's got this. Just watch."

And I do watch. I watch as Catcher begins to circle again, his dark eyes tracking Milan's every movement with predatory focus. I watch as he waits for the perfect moment to strike. I watch as he becomes the weapon that everyone in this warehouse knows he is. This is what he was born to do.

Milan tries again, this time a series of quick jabs that Catcher weaves through with ease. The man is fast, but Catcher is faster. Catcher is better. Catcher is everything Milan is not.

And then Catcher moves. It's a simple movement, a quick combination of punches that catch Milan off guard. The first punch lands on Milan's ribs, the second on his jaw. Milan staggers backward, and I can see the shock on his face. He didn't expect Catcher to be this good. He didn't expect to be outmatched so completely.

The crowd goes wild. They're screaming and cheering, and I find myself on the edge of my seat, completely absorbed in the fight. This is what Catcher does. This is who he is. And watching him, seeing him like this, I understand why he's the undefeated champion. He's a machine. He's unstoppable.

But I'm still scared. Because I know how this ends. I know that one of them won't be walking out of this ring alive. And I'm terrified that it might be him.

The fight continues, and I'm completely mesmerised by Catcher's movement. He's light on his feet for his size, which shocks me. I didn't expect someone so massive to be so agile. He twists and turns, his body moving like water, flowing around Milan's attacks with minimal effort. Milan manages to land a few small hits, but nothing big. Nothing that seems to faze Catcher at all. He just keeps moving, keeps fighting, keeps pushing forward.

Catcher ducks under a wild swing and comes up with a devastating uppercut that catches Milan on the chin. Milan's head snaps back, and for a moment, I think it's over. But Milan recovers, shaking it off, and comes back with a series of rapid-fire punches. Catcher weaves through most of them, but one gets through, catching him on the ribs. He grunts but doesn't slow down. If anything, it makes him angrier.

The crowd is going absolutely insane. They're screaming and cheering, and I find myself on my feet without realising it, my hands in the air as I scream along with everyone else. I'm caught up in the moment, caught up in the violence and the danger and the sheer power of what I'm witnessing.

Then, suddenly, a big burly-looking man runs to the ring edge and starts yelling in a language I don't understand. The words are angry rapid fire, and Milan's eyes flick that way for just a moment. It's only a second of distraction, but in a fight like this, a second is an eternity. A second can mean the difference between life and death.

The man yelling is someone Milan knows; that much is clear. But why is he so angry? More than angry, he looks furious. And now that I'm looking at him more closely, I can see the resemblance. The same shaved head, the same broad shoulders, the same menacing presence. Brothers, maybe. Or family of some kind. Someone important to Milan.

The man storms off, disappearing back into the crowd, but the damage is done. Milan's focus is fractured now, and Catcher sees it. He presses his advantage, moving in with a combination of punches that Milan barely manages to block. Catcher is relentless. He keeps coming, keeps pushing, keeps fighting. He's like a force of nature, unstoppable and inevitable.

I lean over to Gabe and whisper, "Who was that?"

Gabe's jaw is tight, and his eyes are fixed on the ring. "Someone who shouldn't be here," he says quietly. There's a warning in his voice, a hint of something darker.

I don't ask any more questions. I just turn back to the fight and watch as Catcher continues to dominate Milan. The man is good; I can tell that much. But Catcher is better. Catcher is the best. There's no one in this warehouse who can touch him.

Milan tries another combination, and this time he manages to land a solid hit on Catcher's shoulder. Catcher rolls with it, using the momentum to spin and come back with a vicious elbow strike that catches Milan on the side of the head. Milan staggers, and I can see the blood starting to drip from a cut above his eye. It's a small cut, but it's enough. It's a sign of what's to come.

They circle each other again, both breathing hard now. Catcher's chest is heaving, his muscles glistening with sweat. Milan is bleeding and bruised, but he's still fighting. Still trying. Still refusing to go down.

And then Catcher moves in for the kill.

Catcher moves with deadly precision, his body flowing

like liquid violence. He feints left, and when Milan reacts, Catcher comes in with a devastating right hook. It's the knockout hit. Milan's head snaps back, and his body goes limp. He crumples to the mat like a puppet with its strings cut. Like a tree falling in the forest. Like something that was never meant to survive.

I take my seat, my heart pounding in my chest so hard, I think it might burst. Aurelio leans in and covers my eyes with his hand, his voice gentle as he says, "It's over now."

I close my eyes, but I listen as the crowd goes absolutely wild. They're screaming Catcher's name, cheering, roaring their approval. The presenter's voice booms through the warehouse: "And Catcher remains the undefeated champion! Can anyone ever take this man's title away? I doubt it!"

I feel Aurelio's hand move away from my eyes, but I keep them closed. I can't look. I can't see what happens to Milan's body. I can't see the blood and the violence that comes with victory in this world. I don't want to see it. I don't need to see it.

Then I feel his presence before I see him. A heat. A warmth that I've come to recognise as uniquely his. He stands in front of me, and a hand tips my head up from where I'm sitting. I open my eyes to see Catcher standing there, dripping with sweat, his dark eyes boring into mine with an intensity that takes my breath away. He's beautiful. God, he's so beautiful. How is he so beautiful when he's just killed someone?

"Thank you for closing your eyes, little bird," he says, his voice rough and breathless. "We can go home now."

He puts pressure on my chin, enough for me to know I

need to stand. So, I do. I stand on shaky legs and wrap my arms around his sweaty body, leaning up to place my lips on his. I'm so glad he's alive. I'm mortified that I feel this way. Falling for your captor isn't right. That's some Stockholm syndrome shit right there. But I just don't care right now. He's alive. He won. And now that I've seen him fight, I can see why he's undefeated. No one is going to win against this man. No one.

His arms wrap around me as he pulls me tight to him, lifting me off the floor and leaving my legs dangling as he turns and walks toward the change room with me in his arms. I'm pressed against his chest, feeling his heartbeat, feeling the heat of his body, feeling completely safe and completely terrified at the same time.

"Did you miss me, little bird?" he asks, the smile in his voice is muffled by my mouth. "I was only gone for fifteen minutes."

I laugh into his mouth, refusing to stop kissing him. I can't stop kissing him. I don't want to stop kissing him. I want to stay like this forever, suspended in this moment where nothing else matters but him. me and this feeling between us.

He smiles, and says, "Let's get changed and go home."

He places my feet down and grabs my hand, pulling me toward the change room. Gabe and Aurelio trail behind us, talking in what sounds like Italian. I don't understand the words, but I can hear the concern in their voices.

But right now, I don't care about any of that. Right now, all I care about is Catcher. All I care about is the fact that he's alive and he's holding my hand and taking me home.

As we reach the change room, he pulls me close one more time and whispers against my ear, "You were so fucking beautiful watching me fight, little bird. Seeing you there, knowing you were watching me, it made my dick hard."

I blush and bury my face in his chest, he laughs, the sound rumbling through his body and into mine. This man has completely taken over my life. And I'm okay with that. More than okay. I'm thrilled by it.

Chapter 17

Catcher

I open the door and buckle Posey into her seat; my movements deliberate and careful. She's still buzzing from the fight, her energy electric and intoxicating, and I want to make sure she's safe and secure before we head home. I buckle the seatbelt into place, leaning down to kiss her forehead before closing the door and walking around to my side. The scent of her lingers on my skin, sweat, perfume and something uniquely her that I'm becoming addicted to.

I get in and start the car, pulling out of the parking spot and heading toward the exit. The drive home is quiet at first, just the sound of the engine and the occasional sound of traffic. But then Posey speaks up, her curiosity getting the better of her.

"What do they do with the bodies?" she asks, her voice curious and matter of fact.

I frown and glance over at her, slightly amused by the question. "Of all the things I thought you would ask about tonight, you ask that?"

She laughs and says, "Sorry, I just thought it then I got stuck on the thought."

I can't help but smile at her. "Well, we own a crematorium down the road. So, all the people who lose get taken there after each fight. We don't take them all at once, because that's a lot of bodies to take in and out. We do it one by one, and burn them one by one, and mix the ashes in with others during the week."

She grimaces and says, "Gross."

I huff and say, "Yep, but it works well. There's only one fight a week and two to four fights happen, so it's not a lot of bodies that need to be burnt."

"So, you fight weekly? Every week?" she asks, her tone shifting to something more concerned.

"No," I say, shaking my head. "Because we own the club, I get offers to fight, and I go through them and only say yes to ones I think will be worth my time."

"Do you make money on each fight?" she asks, her curiosity piqued.

"Yes," I say simply.

"You must have good odds then," she says.

I laugh at that. "That fight was set to make around five hundred thousand for me if I won."

She gapes at me and says, "Five hundred thousand! Are you kidding me?"

I laugh again. Her French accent gets so thick when she's shocked, and it's so fucking sexy. I want to pull over and kiss her senseless, to taste that shock on her lips.

"Yes, little bird. Five hundred thousand," I say.

She shakes her head and says, "You've had like five

fights since I've known you. That's like what, over two million?"

"Little bird, I'm not poor," I say, laughing again at her incredulity.

"Oh, I got that," she says, "but that's a lot of money."

"Well, yes, it is," I say. "That's why so many people step into the ring. They want the money."

"Do the losing people get anything?" she asks, and I can hear the genuine concern in her voice.

I consider the question for a moment, my hands tightening on the steering wheel. "I've taken a few fights in the past knowing the family had bet against their son I was fighting. Some have stepped into the ring to die to help their family or pay a debt they owe to someone. Sometimes when I know that's what they're doing, I'll take the fight for that very reason; so their death actually means something."

She's quiet for a moment, processing the information and what it means about the world I live in. Then she asks, "So tonight, that man Milan, why did you take that?"

"Because he's an undefeated boxer," I say. "I wanted a challenge. I didn't look into his background, just seen that he himself hadn't lost yet and had been undefeated for about two years, so it looked fun."

She gapes at me and says, "Playing 50-50 with your life is fun?"

I laugh again, she crosses her arms and looks out the window, clearly upset with me. I reach over and place my hand on her thigh, squeezing gently, trying to reassure her.

"You catching feelings, little bird?" I ask, my voice teasing but also sincere.

She doesn't answer, just keeps her eyes fixed on the window. But I can see the blush creeping up her neck, and I know I've hit a nerve. She is catching feelings. And the thought of that makes me very fucking happy. It means she cares. It means she's worried about me. It means she's mine.

I keep my hand on her thigh as I drive, feeling the warmth of her skin through the fabric of her jeans. She doesn't move it away, which tells me everything I need to know. She's caught. Just like I'm caught. We're both trapped in this thing between us, and neither of us is fighting it anymore.

The drive home is quiet after that, but it's not an uncomfortable silence. It's a charged silence, full of unspoken words and emotions that hang between us like electricity. When we finally pull up to the house and I punch in the gate code, I see her watching my fingers again, trying to memorise the numbers. I wonder if she's thinking about running. I wonder if she's thinking about leaving.

The thought makes my chest tight and my stomach twist with a fear I've never felt before. But I push it aside. She's not going anywhere, if I have anything to say about it. Not tonight. Not ever.

I park out the front and turn to her. "Come on, little bird. Let's get inside."

She unbuckles her seatbelt and gets out before I even have a chance to open her door. I'm not impressed. I let her out of the car, not her. I get out of the SUV, my movements sharp and quick, and I storm after her toward the front door. She doesn't realise I'm angry, she probably thinks I'm just eager to get inside, eager to get her alone. But my jaw is clenched, and my hands are curled into fists at my sides.

She reaches the front door and turns around; She sees my face, sees the anger simmering just beneath the surface, and she gasps.. I crowd her against the door, my body pressing hers back against the hard wood, trapping her between me and the unyielding surface.

"You will wait for me to let you out of the car, you hear me, Posey?" I say, my voice low and commanding, with a dark edge she hasn't heard from me before.

She tilts her head back to look at me, her eyes wide with surprise. "Why?"

"Because that's my job," I say. "I open the door. I help you out."

She frowns and says, "I can open a door."

"Oh, I know," I say. "I just saw you do it. But it's my job and you will wait."

I step into her closer, her back now firmly against the front door. "You will wait," I say again, my voice brooking no argument.

She gulps and says, "Okay."

"You are mine; you hear me?" I state, my voice intense. "Mine to protect. Mine to care for. Mine to help. And that," I point back to the car, "is one of the things you'll let me do."

She stammers, "Oh, okay."

I deflate a little, realising I'm being irrational. I know why, too. The thought of her running from me, leaving me, scares me more than anything else in this world. More than death. More than losing a fight. More than anything. I don't want to cage her. I want her to want me, like Alba wants Gabe. Someone who is happy with the cage and chooses to stay willingly.

I lean a little of my weight into her body and say, "Sorry, little bird."

Then I sigh, a long, shaky breath that seems to come from deep within my chest. "This whole thing is confusing for me. I'm not used to this. I'm still hyped up from the fight. I just... I just..."

I can't bring myself to say it, but I want to. I want to tell her that I love her. That I'm terrified of losing her. That she's become everything to me. That the thought of her leaving makes me feel like I'm dying inside.

Her hand snakes up between us and cups my cheek. Leaning my face into her touch, seeking the comfort she's offering. Her skin is soft and warm, and it grounds me.

"It's okay," she says softly. "I get it. I like you too, Catcher. And for me, liking my captor is just fucked up."

"You're not a captive," I say firmly. "I'm not your master. I've told you this."

She says, "Then tell me the code to get out."

I freeze. The words make me ill, and suddenly I can't breathe. She wants the code. She wants to be able to leave. She wants to get out. The thought sends a spike of fear through my entire body.

What if she leaves and doesn't come back?

What if she runs? What if she goes back to France?

I can feel my heart pounding in my chest, my hands shaking. I grip her tighter, pulling her closer, as if I can keep her here through sheer force of will. As if I can make her stay by holding her hard enough.

"Catcher?" she says softly, her voice uncertain. "Are you okay?"

I'm not okay. I'm terrified. I'm absolutely fucking terrified of losing her.

I take a shaky breath and pull her close, kissing her forehead, then her nose, then her lips. The words tumble out of me before I can stop them, raw, vulnerable and absolutely terrifying words.

"I'm scared you won't come back," I say against her mouth. "I'm scared you'll take the code, leave me and never come back."

She pulls back slightly, her eyes searching mine. And I see the realisation dawn on her face. She understands now. She understands that my fear isn't about her escaping. My fear is about her choosing to leave me. My fear is about losing her.

"I'm not going anywhere," she says softly, her hand cupping my face. "I'm scared too, Catcher. I'm scared that you'll go to one of those fights and you won't come back. That you'll die in that ring, and I'll be left here alone."

She's been terrified this whole time. Terrified that I would die. Terrified that I would leave her.

I lean in and kiss her, deep and forcefully, like I'm able to pull her right into my own body and keep her there 24/7. She lets me. She lets me devour her mouth, her lips soft and yielding beneath mine. My hand goes behind her head and pulls her closer, my tongue so deep in her mouth I'm sure I'll feel her tonsils. She moans into the kiss, and the sound drives me absolutely fucking crazy. It's a sound of surrender, of need, of want.

I pick her up, her legs wrapping around my waist as I

use my fingerprint to open the door, and stumble inside with her wrapped around my front. I don't bother taking her anywhere else. I kick the door closed with my foot and simply lay her out on the floor, right inside the front door of the house.

Her top has ridden up a little, showing off her stomach and her abs. Abs on a female are not something I used to find sexy, but on her it's the hottest thing I've ever seen. I wonder what it would look like round with my kid, because that's exactly what I'm going to do. I'm going to fill her belly with my baby. She can't leave then. She'll be bound to me forever. The thought makes me feral and completely fucking obsessed.

I've not used protection with her once, which should have been the biggest indicator to me that I was completely wrapped up in her. It's something I've never once not used. I was never going to be trapped with a kid. But with Posey, it has never been a thought. I just came inside her time and again, and it never crossed my mind to stop. She hasn't asked either, so she's as gone as I am, or she's protected somehow.

I look along her body laid out before me on the floor. She watches me with a look that says, *"Um, are you going to touch me?"*

All I say is, "Why haven't you asked me for a condom, Posey?"

I can hear the accusation in my own voice as I say it.

She frowns and says, "I'm on the shot. Why?"

Chapter 18

Posey

Catcher's eyes darken as he looks at me, spread out on the floor. The intensity in his gaze is almost too much to bear, but I can't look away. I'm a mess of tangled limbs and raw desire, and he's the architect of it all.

"How long does it last?" he asks, his voice a low growl that vibrates through the floor and into my body, a primal sound that makes my core clench in anticipation.

"Three months," I manage to whisper, my breath catching in my throat. The words feel insignificant against the weight of his stare.

"And how long does yours have left?" he presses, his eyes never leaving mine.

I swallow hard, the reality of my situation hitting me even in this haze of lust. "About two weeks or so."

He smirks, a slow, curve of his lips that promises both pleasure and danger. "Good."

Good? What the fuck. Not good, I think, the last vestiges of my rational mind screaming a warning, but he smothers my mouth with his before I can say anything back. This man is so feral right now. He got all worked up because I opened my own door, for fuck's sake. A door. Like, umm, what the hell. The absurdity of his possessiveness is almost as intoxicating as his kiss.

He continues to kiss me until my mind goes blank and my own hands reach for him, desperate to feel the solid reality of him. I unbutton his top, running my hands along the hard ridges of his chest. Gods, he is strong. There isn't an ounce of fat on this man, and there should be. I've seen him eat, the way he can devour three containers of food in one sitting. I know I can easily put away food when I'm training, but three containers is a lot. He's a machine, built for consumption and destruction, and I'm fascinated by the sheer, brutal efficiency of him.

Catcher's hands are roaming my body now too, slowly pulling my top up over my breasts and pulling my breasts free from the bra I'm wearing. His eyes zero in on my breasts when they spill free, his pupils blowing wide before he leans in to take each one in his mouth until they are so hard it's painful. He loves to play with the peaks he makes there, flicking them with his tongue, sucking them deep into his mouth. The sensation is electric, a jolt of pure pleasure that makes me arch my back against the cold floor, a silent plea for more.

Then his hands are finding my jeans and undoing them, the zipper a harsh sound in the quiet house. He pulls them down my legs, leaving me in my underwear. His finger brushes what must be a damp spot there now, and I gasp at the contact, the sudden, sharp awareness of my own need.

He leans down, his voice a low, filthy whisper against

my ear. "Your pussy weeps so well for me, you know this, right? It weeps knowing I'm going to stuff it full of my dick."

I whimper at his dirty words, the sound catching in my throat. He slowly peels my underwear down, his eyes locked with mine, a silent question and a demand. "Do you want me to stuff you, Posey? Fill you up so good your belly bulges from it? Want to see my dick moving inside you? I know I do. I love seeing you stuffed." His words are a heavy, velvet rope, binding me to him.

He lowers his face to my pussy, a hungry look on his face as he buries his face there and breathes in deep. He does this every time he licks me, just breathes me in deeply, as if trying to memorise my scent, to claim me with his very breath. I cannot imagine what it smells like down there, but he is feral for it. As his fingers spread my folds, his tongue darts out to taste me. He growls when I hit his tongue and he says, "You taste like mine... you know that. You taste like you belong to me."

Then he eats. Fuck me, Catcher can eat pussy like a porn star. He nibbles and sucks at my clit and sinks two of his fat fingers inside me, then three. Lately, he has been adding a fourth as he says, his voice muffled against my skin, "One day, Posey, you will take it all. One day, you will be so stretched wide, I'll be able to fit it all in." The promise of his size, the promise of that complete fullness, makes my breath hitch.

He pumps away at my pussy, the stretch feeling amaz-ing. I had no idea sex could be like this. This is my favourite type, this dirty, filthy version that Catcher gives. His fingers speed up, and my orgasm crashes through me. I clench down on his fingers, my body convulsing, and he continues to fuck me through it, his fingers relentless, driving me deeper into the pleasure.

As soon as I'm done, he leans up and undoes his own pants and pulls his clothes off, his eyes never leaving me. I lean up on my elbows to watch the show, because that's what this is, a show for me, like a striptease, because Catcher's body is perfection. Every tattoo, every scar, every hard line of muscle is a testament to the life he's lived, and I'm mesmerised.

I stare at Catcher's face and see his lip cut has reopened, and he has blood smeared on his face; which is now all over my pussy. Why do I find that hot? It shouldn't be, but it is. The sight of his blood, the evidence of his violence, mixed with the proof of my pleasure, is a dark, intoxicating cocktail.

Catcher grabs his dick and slowly settles between my thighs on the floor and says to me, "Watch yourself stretch to take me, Posey."

So, I do. I look down as he slowly sinks into me, a little bit at a time, his massive dick sinking into me is the hottest thing I've ever seen. The slow, agonising stretch is exquisite, a pain that is pure pleasure. Then he says to me, "I'm gonna keep you, Posey. You're gonna be mine forever, okay?"

And for a second, he looks almost vulnerable, like he wants me to stay with him, choose him. Do I? I'm not sure. Being caged isn't fun, but I don't think I can leave him now. The thought of a life without this intensity, without this man, is a cold empty void.

He leans down till our foreheads are touching, and he says, "Please choose this, Posey."

Then he starts to fuck me slowly, and I'm a panting mess. I'm so full of him, his words, his dick. I tilt my head back as he slowly goes a bit faster and let the sensations just flow over me. I wrap my legs around his waist, pulling him deeper, wanting to feel every inch of him inside me. I want to be filled with him. I want to be claimed by him.

He starts to fuck me harder. I can feel my lower back being thrust into the floor. It hurts, but it heightens the pleasure. Go figure, right? Catcher's mouth covers mine again, his whole body covering mine now. His hands scoop under my shoulders and grab onto the top of them as he starts to thrust hard and deep, each one hitting that spot inside me, making me see stars. I start to come, my pussy clamping down, as he growls in my ears, "Fuck, Posey, you are perfect."

Then I let go, my orgasm washing over me completely. He comes too, and I can feel his hot cum coating my walls inside me. Catcher's mouth finds mine again as he kisses me slow and deep. It almost feels tender and loving; if a captor could love his captive.

He pulls back and stares into my eyes as he says, "Choose to stay and I'll let you be free."

I look at him, my heart pounding in my chest. The paradox of his words is almost too much to bear. Choose to stay to be free. It's the most Catcher thing he could ever say. And I know, deep down, that he means it. He's giving me the ultimate choice.

I smile, a slow, genuine smile that reaches my eyes. "I

choose you, Catcher." I don't think I had another choice really, he made it hard to not choose him.

Chapter 19

Catcher

I wake to the weight of her.

It's a good weight, a grounding kind of weight; a weight I never knew I craved until it settled over me. Posey is a small, compact furnace curled into my side, her body a perfect, yielding curve against the hard, unyielding line of mine. My arm is a dead, heavy thing pinned beneath her neck, and my other arm is draped over her waist like a thick protective band. One of my legs is thrown over hers, anchoring her to the mattress, to me, and to this moment.

The first, panicked thought that always hits me when I wake up with her is a cold spike of fear: Did I smother her? I'm too big, too rough, too much man for this beautiful thing. I shift my head slightly, and a soft, warm puff of air fans across my chest, right over my heart. She's breathing. A slow, steady rhythm that is the only proof I need that the world is still turning.

A thin, slick layer of sweat coats the space between us.

The air in the room is already thick and heavy, the kind of oppressive heat that promises a scorching Melbourne day.

I crack open one eye. The blinds are wide open, just as I left them last night in my haste to get her into our bed. The morning sun, now high and brutal, streams through the window, cutting golden, dusty paths across the floor. It's blinding, and I know instantly it's later than I ever allow myself to sleep. My internal clock is usually a merciless warden, dragging me out of sleep before the first hint of dawn. But today, the warden is silent.

It's my day off. Gabe always insists on it, the day after a fight is sacred. A day for healing, for quiet, for letting the adrenaline drain out of the system. I usually spend it alone, nursing bruises and staring at the ceiling. Now, I spend it with her.

I look down at the crown of her head, the dark, messy spill of her hair against my shoulder. Her scent, a mix of perfume she got at the chemist, sweat, and the sharp, coppery tang of sex, is intoxicating. It's a scent that has burrowed deep into my brain, creating a new kind of home.

A familiar, domestic impulse surfaces, soft and strange. I wonder if she's hungry. I wonder if she'd like to go to Woolworths again. The last time, she walked the aisles with a quiet, almost childlike wonder, picking out anything she wanted. It was a mundane, normal thing, and it felt like the most dangerous, revolutionary act I'd ever committed. Taking a girl I'd essentially kidnapped to buy groceries.

Then the memory hits me, a cold, hard fist to the gut, shattering the fragile peace of the morning.

"Choose to stay and I'll let you free."

The words I spoke last night, thick with lust and a terrifying, unprecedented vulnerability, echo in the quiet room. I offered her the key to her own cage. I offered her the choice to walk away from the man who has claimed her, body and soul.

Do I have the capacity to give her the gate code?

The question is a tremor in my chest, a betrayal of everything I am. I am Catcher. I take what I want. I keep what is mine. I don't offer freedom. I offer a gilded cage, a comfortable prison, but a prison, nonetheless. Yet I did. I saw the fear in her eyes, the defiance that still flickered there, and I knew the only way to truly break her, or, God help me, to truly keep her, is to give her the power to leave.

I have to know. I have to see if the caged bird stays, even when the door is open.

She said she chooses me. *"I choose you, Catcher."* Her voice, a husky whisper with that soft, beautiful French accent, was the sweetest sound I've ever heard. It was a victory more profound than any I've ever won in the ring.

But does she? Does she choose the man who dragged her out of a hellhole and then kept her captive in his isolated bush property? Does she choose the violence, the darkness, the possessiveness that is woven into the very fabric of my being? Or does she choose the fleeting tenderness, the moments of connection, the brutal, honest sex?

My heart, usually a steady, slow drum, starts pumping hard and fast. I feel a panic rising, a desperate, animal urge to clamp down, to retract the offer, to lock the doors and throw away the key.

I need to move. I need to break the contact.

With agonising slowness, I begin to untangle myself. My arm, numb and heavy, slides out from under her neck. I lift my leg, careful not to jostle her. Every movement is a calculated risk, a fear that if I wake her, I'll have to face the choice, face the questions in her eyes.

Posey doesn't stir. She just rolls onto her stomach, burrowing her face into the pillow where my head was, her hand instinctively reaching out for the warmth I've left behind. She is a creature of comfort, of instinct, and in this moment, her instinct is to cling to the space I occupied.

I pull myself from the bed, the mattress sighing softly in protest. The air hits my skin, and I feel suddenly exposed, naked in the bright sunlight. I grab a pair of dark grey athletic shorts from the floor, pulling them on with jerky impatient movements.

I look back at her one last time. She is utterly beautiful, utterly mine, and utterly free to leave. The thought is a poison and an elixir all at once.

I turn and head downstairs. The house is silent, the only sound the soft thud of my bare feet on the wooden stairs. I walk into the kitchen, the cold tile a welcome shock against my feet, as I pressing the button on the reverse cycle aircon to try and cool the house down before it gets too hot.

The espresso machine sits on the counter, a sleek, black monument to my pre-Posey routine. It's hardly been used since she arrived. Every morning, I find myself making a pot of Earl Grey or some herbal blend, sitting across from her as we sip tea together. It's a soft, domestic ritual I've grown accustomed to, a quiet moment of peace I never knew I needed. But today, I don't want soft. I need the hard, bitter jolt of caffeine. I need to be sharp, to be Catcher, to face the terrifying reality of the choice I've given her.

I grind the beans, the whirring sound a violent comfort in the quiet house. I warm the milk, the steam a soft cloud against my face. I make myself a latte, the layers of dark espresso, warm milk, and light foam.

I stand there, staring at the polished granite countertop, the warmth of the mug seeping into my palms. The choice. I have to make it real.

I find a small, yellow sticky note tucked into a drawer. I grab a pen and press the tip hard against the paper. My hand is steady, but my heart is not as I write the code, the six digits that control the only way out of this property; the only barrier between her and the world.

228437

I pause, the pen hovering. I can't just leave the number. It needs context.

I write the message, the words coming out as a twisted version of a love note, a declaration of care.

Posey,
This is the gate code, please remember if you leave, you need a bodyguard.
So, please just tell me before so I can arrange one, and someone to drive you.

I look at the note. Its a threat and a promise, a cage and a key. It's perfect. Then, on a sudden, ridiculous impulse, I draw a wonky looking heart at the bottom. It's lopsided and childish, but I tired. I stare at it, a slow, self-mocking smile pulling at my lips. For me, maybe it is a love note. A confession from a scared heart.

I take my coffee, the mug warm and heavy, and walk out the back door. The wrap-around porch is already bathed in sunlight as I walk down the steps and settle into the chair that Posey sits in daily.

She calls it her ten minutes of sun. She's a creature of the shade, a girl who spent too long in the dark, but she insists on this ritual. I don't oppose it. Her skin now has a more Australian glow to it than it did when she first got here, browner now, rather than golden; it really suits her pretty face. A few freckles have also bloomed across the bridge of her nose, tiny, dark constellations that make her even more attractive than she was to start with. She's becoming a part of this place, a part of my world.

I settle into the seat, the wicker creaking softly under my weight. I watch the world outside my fence line. A small mob of kangaroos is dotted across the clearing, grazing lazily. The birds are loud today, their calls sharp and insistent in the thick morning air.

I just sit. I sit with my feelings, with the bitter taste of the coffee, and the terrifying, scared heart that beats beneath my ribs. I really want her to stay. I want her to wake up, find the note, and choose to burn it. I want her to choose the cage I've built for her, because it's the only place I know how to keep her safe. The choice is hers. And I have to wait. I have to wait and see if the choice she made in the heat of the moment holds true in the cold light of day.

Chapter 20

Posey

I surface slowly, dragged from a deep, dreamless sleep by the relentless birds. My body feels heavy, and deliciously sated; the dull ache in my muscles a sweet reminder of the night before. I stretch, reaching for the solid warmth that should be beside me, but my hand only meets empty sheet.

My eyes snap open. The space next to me is cold. Not just cool, but truly cold; the kind of cold that means Catcher has been gone for a long time. A small, sharp pang of disappointment hits me, quickly followed by a familiar, unwelcome anxiety. Where is he?

I sit up, the sheet pooling around my waist. The room is flooded with a harsh light, the brilliant glare making me squint. I walk to the window, my bare feet silent on the floor. The sun is high, almost directly overhead. Mon Dieu, what time is it? I never sleep this late.

I look out over the backyard. The sight that greets me is both a relief and a confusion. There he is. Catcher. He's sitting in the backyard, in my chair, the wicker one I drag out for my ten minutes of sun. He's massive, a dark, imposing silhouette against the bright green of the Australian bush. He's just sitting, still and silent, staring out at the fence line. He looks like a king surveying his kingdom, or perhaps a guard watching his prison.

A wave of warmth washes over me, chasing away the chill of the empty bed.

I turn away from the window, the need for the bathroom suddenly urgent. I use the bathroom, splash cold water on my face, and then head back to my bedroom. I'm still naked, and the air-conditioned chill of the house raises goosebumps on my skin.

I open the wardrobe, my eyes scanning the limited but growing collection of clothes he's provided. Today, I choose my training clothes. I need the feel of the familiar, the comfort of the routine. I pull on the purple set; tight shorts that hug my thighs and a matching sports bra-like top. It stops just above my belly button. The top is designed for someone with a much larger chest, all thick straps and industrial-strength support. I don't need the support, not really, but I love the feeling of being held, of being contained. It's a strange comfort, a parallel to the life I'm living now.

Dressed, I feel a shift in my mood, returning to the quiet strength I've been cultivating. I head downstairs, the scent of stale coffee and something sweet lingering in the air.

I walk into the kitchen and go straight for the kettle. I flip the switch, the sudden, rumble of the water beginning to boil a comforting sound. As I wait, I reach up and pull my hair into a high, tight ponytail, the elastic snapping against my scalp. I grab my favourite mug and pot, placing a tea bag inside it.

Then, I turn and lean back against the counter, placing my hands flat on the cool, smooth surface of the bench. I'm waiting for the water to boil, but my eyes are drawn to a small, bright spot of yellow on the counter.

A sticky note.

My breath catches in my throat. I know, instinctively, what it is.

I reach out a trembling hand and pull the pad toward me. The paper is slightly curled at the edges, and I can see the indentations of his heavy handwriting.

Posey,
This is the gate code, please remember if you leave, you need a bodyguard.
So, please just tell me before so I can arrange one, and someone to drive you.

And below the text, a small, wonky-looking heart.

My eyes lock onto the six digits above the text: 228437.

He actually did it. He gave me the code. The key. The absolute, undeniable proof that the cage door is open. I stare at the numbers, then at the heart, then back at the numbers. The message is so Catcher, a demand wrapped in a promise, a threat disguised as care. If you leave, you need a bodyguard. He can't even let me go without trying to control the terms of my freedom.

A strange, dizzying mix of emotions washes over me: shock, a flicker of fear, and a profound, unexpected tenderness. The wonky heart is what breaks me. It's so vulnerable, so out of character for the grim reaper who owns this house. Its a twisted love note, a confession of his own scared heart, just as much as it is a gate code.

I pull the note off the pad, the sticky bit making a small, tearing sound. I walk over to the fridge, my eyes still scanning the numbers, trying to etch them into my memory. I find a magnet, a ridiculous, brightly coloured souvenir from a place I don't recognise and press the note firmly onto the stainless-steel door. It's for added security, a commitment to the reality of the choice.

I will need to remember those numbers. I am terrible with numbers, with codes, with anything that doesn't require rote memorisation. But if I read it every day, if I see it every time I reach for the milk, it will stick. It has to.

The kettle clicks off, the sudden silence jarring. I pour the boiling water over the tea bag, the steam rising in a fragrant cloud. I let it steep for a moment, then pour some into my cup, adding a splash of milk from the fridge. As I do, I mumble the code to myself, trying to memorise it. "Two-two-eight-four-three-seven." I repeat it again, the numbers feeling clumsy and foreign on my tongue.

I grab my cup, the warmth seeping into my hands, and head for the back door. The choice is real. The freedom is real. But as I look at the numbers, and then out the window at the massive, silent man sitting in my chair, I realise something profound. I made my choice last night, in the heat of the moment, and I meant it.

I walk out the door, down the porch steps, and right out to where he sits. He's so engrossed in watching the bush that he doesn't hear me until I'm directly in his sight line.

He looks up, his eyes, usually so hard and guarded, soften as they land on me. A slow, genuine smile spreads across his face; a rare but beautiful thing that makes my heart flutter. He turns his body slightly, a silent invitation, and I settle into his lap.

His lap is hard, a solid shelf of muscle and bone, but it's the most comfortable place in the world. I curl into him; the mug of tea held carefully in my hands. He wraps a heavy arm around my waist, pulling me tight against his body.

"Morning," he murmurs, his voice a low rumble against my ear. He nuzzles his face into the side of my neck, his stubble scratching my skin in a way that sends a shiver of pleasure through me.

"Bonjour," I reply, the French word slipping out naturally.

He pulls back just enough to look at me, a mischievous glint in his eyes. "Bonjour," he copies, his accent thick and clumsy, making me laugh.

"You want to go to Woolworths again today?" he asks, his thumb stroking the skin just above the waistband of my shorts.

"Oh, yes please," I say, a genuine smile on my face. Then I push my luck, wanting to test the boundaries of this new, fragile freedom. "Can we also go for lunch? I would really like to go out for lunch."

I watch his face, waiting for the flicker of control, the tightening of his jaw that signals the cage door slamming shut. He hesitates for a beat, his eyes searching mine.

Then I think 'fuck it' and say the one thing that has

been nagging at me about the note. "Can I also, maybe, have a phone?"

He goes completely still. His body, which was soft and yielding a moment ago, turns to stone. He is a rock, unmoving, and the change is immediate and terrifying.

"Why?" he asks, the single word clipped and dangerous.

I keep my voice steady, my logic clear. "You said I need a guard to go out. How do I contact you to get one if you're not home? If I'm out, and I need to call you, I cannot."

At that, his body softens, the tension bleeding out of him in a slow, visible wave. He relaxes against the chair, his arm tightening around me. "I didn't think of that," he admits, the admission of oversight a small victory. "Okay, Posey. You can have a phone."

I know he will monitor the phone like a hawk. Every call, every text, every app will be under his scrutiny. But in reality, I have no one to call anyway. My old life is gone, and the people in it are either dead or complicit in my sale. But it will be nice to be able to contact Catcher if I need to. It's a lifeline, a connection to the only person I know now.

He pulls me closer to his body, the coffee on the arm of the chair now completely cold and forgotten. He squeezes me against him, a silent claim.

"We can go out for lunch. We can go to Woolworths, and we can get you a phone, Posey."

I smile, a deep, contented feeling settling in my chest. I look out at the view, at the kangaroos grazing in the distance.

"Those creatures are so scary," I note, a small shiver running through me.

He chuckles, the sound deep and rich. "They can be very scary, Posey. But I promise you, they are not going to hurt you. Nothing will hurt you with me around."

I lean my head against his chest, listening to the steady, powerful beat of his heart. The words are a promise, a vow, and a threat all rolled into one. And I find I like it.

Chapter 21

Catcher

I watch her walk out the door, and the sight of her nearly stops my heart.

She's not in the purple training gear anymore. She changed after the quick training session we had. I love training with her. She's a natural, a coiled spring of muscle and instinct; her power a beautiful and terrifying thing to behold. We worked the heavy bag, then some light sparring, she moved with a ferocity that makes me truly hope, that one day she might take me up on the idea of a few professional fights. She has the build, the drive, and the raw, unbridled aggression. I could make her a champion.

Now, she's dressed for the city. Black slacks that skim her hips and fall perfectly to her ankles, and a crisp, white blouse that buttons high on her neck, a stark, elegant contrast to her dark hair and sun-kissed skin. The outfit is simple, classic, and utterly captivating. It's a quiet kind of power, a different kind of weapon than the one she wields in the ring, but just as effective.

We walk side-by-side to the car, my hand touching her lower back as I open the passenger door for her; a small unnecessary gesture that still feels important. She slides in without a word; a ghost of a smile plays on her lips. She knows I'm watching her, waiting for the moment she might reach for the handle herself, but she doesn't. She's playing my game, and I find I like it.

"Lunch first," I tell her when I slide into my side of the car, pulling the heavy door shut. "We'll do the Woolworths shop on the way home. Don't want the food to spoil."

She nods, buckling her seatbelt. "Lunch in the city, yes? I am excited." Her accent makes the word excited sound like a promise.

Her excitement is a balm to my raw nerves. I start the engine, the low growl of the V8 a familiar comfort. I pull the SUV out of the driveway and head toward the main gate.

As we approach the keypad, I slow the car. I lean forward, my body instinctively shielding the code from her view, even though she already knows it. The action is a reflex, a habit born of years of paranoia and secrecy, but it feels like a betrayal of the choice I offered her. I punch in the numbers, the same numbers now stuck to my fridge, and the heavy steel gate begins to slide open with a low, grinding sound.

I glance at her as we drive through. She's not even looking at the keypad. She's looking ahead, out at the road, at the world I'm taking her back into.

I take a deep breath, the air thick with the scent of eucalyptus and dry summer grass. My mind flashes back to the kitchen, to the yellow square on the stainless steel.

She saw it. She read it. She put it on the fridge. And she didn't run.

She didn't take the key and bolt. She didn't use the code to escape. She stuck it up like a reminder, a promise, and then she asked for lunch. She asked for more time with me.

She didn't run. She chose to stay.

It's a victory, a monumental, soul-shaking win, but the relief is tempered by a cold, hard realism. She chose me in the quiet of the house, in the warmth of my arms. Now, I'm taking her back out into the world, into the city, into the heart of my territory. Only time will tell if that choice holds up when the cage door is truly open, when the noise and the crowds and the possibility of escape are all around her.

I'm taking her to the casino. Not to the main floor, not to the noise and the smoke and the desperate energy of the gamblers. I'm taking her to the top.

Gabe owns the place. It's a fortress, a legitimate front for a thousand illegitimate dealings. But it also has a private room on the top floor, a space I've only used a handful of times. It's all glass, overlooking the entire city of Melbourne and the gambling floors below. From up there, the world looks small, manageable, and utterly under our control.

I called Gabe this morning, right after she asked for lunch. He didn't even question it. Just a grunt of acknowledgment and a promise that the room would be set, the food prepared, and the staff sworn to silence. Twelve o'clock. It's a power move, a declaration of ownership, but it's also the only way I can ensure her safety and my peace of mind. I can't risk taking her to a public restaurant, not with the way she looks, not with the enemies I have.

As we drive, I glance over at her. She's watching the city come into view, her expression thoughtful.

"Where are we going?" she asks, her voice soft.

"A place with a view," I tell her, keeping my answer deliberately vague. "A place where no one can bother us."

She smiles, a genuine, open smile that makes my gut clench. "A place where you can keep an eye on me, n'est-ce pas?"

I don't deny it. I just reach over and take her hand, my thumb tracing the strong bones of her wrist. "Always, Posey. Always."

The drive is long, the transition from the isolated bush to the urban sprawl of Melbourne a jarring one. The air thickens, the sounds multiply, and the world becomes a dangerous, chaotic place again. I feel the familiar tension coil in my shoulders, the need to be vigilant, to be Catcher.

I pull the SUV into the VIP parking area, the reserved spot only available to us. The air in the underground garage is cool. The silence is broken only by the soft hum of the ventilation system and the distant clatter of the casino floor.

I cut the engine and step out, the sound of my door closing echoing throughout the concrete space. I walk around the front of the car cand open Posey's door for her. It's a habit now, a small act of service that I find myself enjoying.

Three valet attendants are standing nearby, but they know better than to approach. They're trained to be invisible, especially when I'm around. My car is a fortress, and no one outside my immediate circle is allowed to touch it.

Almost instantly, two figures detach themselves from the shadows. They're my security, dressed in sharp black suits, earpieces discreetly tucked into their ears.

"Mr Calcone," one of them says, his voice a low, professional monotone.

I toss him the keys. They've learned the hard way. At the fight club, the car is parked right at the door, under the direct watch of a dozen men. Here, deep in the underground parking, it needs a dedicated guard. One of the security men will park the car in a secure bay and stay with it, ensuring no one gets near it. It's a necessary precaution.

The second security man, a massive, silent shadow named Marco, stays with us. He walks a respectful two paces ahead, clearing a path that doesn't need clearing, his presence a heavy, undeniable shield.

Posey is taking it all in. Her eyes are wide, flicking from the security guards to the polished concrete, to the distant lights of the casino floor. She's not scared, not exactly, but she's observing, absorbing the new reality I'm presenting to her.

We walk through a maze of corridors, past service elevators and locked doors, until we reach the main casino floor. The sudden blast of noise and light is jarring, the relentless electronic jingle of the slot machines, the low roar of the crowd, the clatter of chips.

As we step onto the edge of the floor, Posey's hand reaches out, her fingers brushing against my wrist. I take her hand instantly, lacing my fingers through hers. Her grip is a little stiff, a small, involuntary tension that tells me she's uneasy, but she doesn't pull away. She's anchoring herself to me, and the satisfaction that floods me is immense.

Marco leads us to a private elevator, the doors opening with a soft chime. The ride up is silent, the only sound the gentle whoosh of the air conditioning. I keep my eyes on Posey, watching the subtle shift in her expression as the noise fades and the tension in her hand begins to ease.

When the doors open, we step out into a world of hushed luxury. Marco gestures toward a set of double doors, then melts back into the shadows near the elevator.

Posey lets go of my hand. The sudden absence of her touch is a cold shock, but I watch as she walks past the set table and the awaiting waiter, drawn by the light. She walks straight to the massive, floor-to-ceiling glass wall that overlooks the entire casino.

She stands there, a small, elegant figure silhouetted against the bright city skyline. She places her hands flat on the cool glass; her gaze fixed on the miniature world below. The main floor is a hive of activity, a frantic, desperate ballet of people chasing luck. I can see the roulette tables spinning, the rows of slot machines blinking, the tiny figures of gamblers hunched over their games.

She's mesmerised. She doesn't speak, just watches as her breath fogs a small circle on the glass.

I walk up behind her, placing my hands on her shoulders, my chin resting on the top of her head. I know what she's seeing. The raw, exposed need of humanity, the ugly truth of people when they think no one is watching.

"Do you want to go downstairs?" I ask, the question a

formality. I wouldn't take her down there. It's a security nightmare, a place where too many eyes would be on her, too many hands would want to touch. It's unsafe. But I need to know her answer. I need to know if the choice I gave her extends to this.

She turns her head slightly, her cheek brushing against my jaw. "Oh, no. That's fine," she says, her voice soft, almost a whisper. "It's very busy."

Then, she admits the truth, a small, vulnerable confession that makes my grip on her shoulders tighten. "I don't like crowds. They make me uneasy."

She turns fully in my arms, looking up at me, her eyes clear and honest. "But I do like to watch them through a window. It's interesting to see what people do when no one is looking."

A slow smile spreads across my face. She sees the world the way I do, from a distance, with a cold, analytical eye. She's a watcher, a student of human nature, just like me.

"Then we will watch," I say, my voice a low growl. "We will watch the world from up here, where it can't touch you."

A soft cough breaks the silence. I turn my head slightly. The waiter, a young man in a crisp uniform, is standing a respectful distance away, his eyes lowered.

"Lunch will be served in five minutes, Mr. Calcone," he says softly, his voice barely a whisper.

"Thank you," I reply, my voice a low rumble as I give him a curt nod, and he retreats; his footsteps silent on the thick carpet.

I guide Posey away from the glass, my hand resting

lightly on the small of her back, leading her to the table. It's set for two, with a pristine white tablecloth, gleaming silverware, and a single, elegant orchid in the centre. Even from the table, you can still see the casino floor below, and her eyes remain trained on the glass wall, on the tiny figures moving within the chaos.

We sit down, and I lean forward, my elbows on the table, my gaze fixed on her.

"You seemed okay at the fight club when I took you," I observe, the question hanging in the air. "How come you seem more stiff here than there?"

She doesn't look away from the window, her brow furrowed in thought. "My father didn't really allow me out much," she begins, her voice quiet. "But he always took me to the fights so he could bet. They feel safe to me. Places like this don't."

She finally turns to me, her eyes earnest. "Maybe I will feel safer with time. It's more than likely just because it's something I never had a chance to experience when I was growing up, but for now it makes me nervous."

I smile, a genuinely easy smile that only she seems to pull from me. "It's the same for me, little bird. I'm not a big fan of crowds, because I can't see who is coming for me. But the fight club and the night club we sometimes frequent are okay; it might just be because we control the narrative at those places."

She smiles back, a flash of understanding in her eyes. "So, why did we come here?"

"Because Gabe owns the place," I explain. "And I control everything when I come. Every camera, every staff member, every security detail is under my control. It was the safest option for us to have a private lunch in the city."

She considers this, then asks. "Why no security when we go to Woolworths?"

"Because it's a small town shopping centre there," I tell her, my hand reaching across the table to cover hers. "And I can protect you in that environment. I can see everything. But if you were to go alone, without me, you would have two to four security guards go with you."

She raises her perfectly sculpted brows, a look of surprise on her face. "That many?"

"Yes," I confirm. "Gabe's wife, Alba, has four to six every time she goes out. At first, she hated it, but there was an incident a few weeks back, and now she will not leave the house without them."

Posey's eyes widen, a genuine concern in their depths. "What happened?"

I hesitate for a moment, weighing how much to tell her. She's part of this world now, and she needs to know the dangers.

"Well, Alba has a complicated past," I say, keeping the short version clean. "But the short version is after Gabe got her back, she went out one day without the guards and was nearly kidnapped by two men who used to work for Gabe. But she was outside of one of the places that Gabe owns, so his men came running out to help her."

I squeeze her hand. "She loves to go shopping, but she's scared to go out much now."

"Oh, dear," Posey whispers, her voice thick with sympathy. "And she went shopping for me?"

I nod, a soft smile touching my lips. "As I said, she loves to shop, so she was grateful for being forced out."

Posey's eyes light up. "I would love to meet her one day."

"I'll arrange it soon," I promise. It's another step, another tether to this new life. She's not just choosing me; she's choosing my world. And I will make sure that world is safe for her.

Chapter 22

Posey

I put my fork down with a soft clink against the porcelain plate. The sound echoes in the sudden silence of the private room, a small punctuation mark on the end of a perfect meal. The food was incredible, rich, complex, and utterly unlike anything I've eaten since I arrived in Australia. I feel a deeply satisfying warmth spread through my belly; a contentment that is both physical and emotional.

"Wow," I breathe out, leaning back in the plush chair, the leather cool against my arms. "That was really good."

Catcher smiles, a slow curve to his lips that makes my heart do a quick, nervous flip. He's been watching me the entire time, not with scrutiny, but with a quiet, intense pleasure that makes me feel cherished; like a rare and beautiful object he's just acquired.

"Did you enjoy it, little bird?" he asks, his voice low, the pet name a soft, familiar brand.

"Very much so." I look around the opulent, silent room, the glass walls reflecting the city's endless sprawl, then back at him. "Have you ever done this before? Taken someone to lunch like this?"

He shakes his head, picking up his wine glass, swirling the deep red liquid. "No."

The simple, blunt answer shocks me. I lean forward, my curiosity piqued, with a sudden fierce need to understand the man across from me. "Why not?"

He shrugs, a massive, indifferent movement that speaks of a lifetime of casual disregard for convention. "Had no need for it. If I wanted company, I would get it. Then I would leave it. I was never one for keeps or effort. Just fleeting fun."

The words are a cold splash of reality. Fleeting fun. Is that what I was supposed to be. That's what he was used to. The thought causes a sharp, unexpected pain.

I raise a brow, a challenge in my eyes, a defiance I can't suppress. "And yet, you kept me without even knowing me."

His smile widens, a gleam entering his eyes that promises both danger and devotion. "I know. I knew from the moment I saw you that you were mine."

The sheer possessiveness and unshakeable conviction in his tone, sends a wave of heat through me. My belly suddenly full of a frantic, beautiful fluttering, as I feel the blush creeping up my neck and across my cheeks. It's ridiculous, this reaction, this schoolgirl flush, but I can't stop it. He makes me feel special; chosen in a way no one ever has.

"I love when you blush," he says, his voice dropping to a low growl, his eyes fixed on the rising colour in my skin. "Your skin blushes so well."

I smile, a genuine, unguarded smile as I push my chair back and stand up, drawn once again to the massive window. I look down at the casino floor, the tiny figures still moving in their frantic dance, their lives playing out in miniature below us.

I need to ask. I need to know. I need to shatter the perfect, fragile bubble of this moment and face the truth.

"Do you plan on not keeping me one day?" I ask, my voice barely a whisper, my gaze fixed on the world below. "Or will you keep me forever?"

I hear the scrape of his chair as he stands. His footsteps are silent on the thick carpet as he comes up behind me. I feel the heat of his body, the solid, comforting presence of him, a wall of muscle and certainty.

His arms wrap around my waist, pulling me back against his chest. "Forever, Posey."

The word is a vow, a promise, a chain. It's everything I want and everything I fear.

I gather my courage, the question a sharp, painful lump in my throat. "Will you still look for fleeting moments with others?"

My voice is vulnerable, thin; asking him if this, us, is a real thing. If he plans to use me like a sex slave while fucking other people, or if I will actually be his. His one and only.

He goes utterly still. Then, he turns me in his arms to face him. His eyes are dark, intense, searching mine, demanding honesty.

"It's just you, Posey," he says, his voice rough with sincerity, a deep resonant sound that vibrates throughout my bones. "I gave you the code to the gate. I trust you. I want you and only you. What do I need to do for you to understand that?"

I look at him, the sincerity in his eyes almost overwhelming. "I don't know," I admit, the words a shaky exhale.

A slow, knowing smirk spreads across his face. "The green-eyed monster looks good on you."

I frown, confused. "I don't understand."

"You're jealous," he states, the simple truth of it making me flush again.

I meet his gaze, refusing to back down. "Yes," I say, the word a defiant whisper.

He laughs, a deep, rumbling sound that vibrates through my chest. "Posey, I would marry you tomorrow if you wanted. In fact, I'll arrange it."

My eyes bug out of my head. Marriage? The word hangs in the air, massive and impossible.

"Hang on! Slow down, baby!" I say, my voice suddenly thick with shock, my hands pushing against his chest. "It's been a couple of months, Catcher, that's it! Just relax."

He leans in, his mouth finding mine in a slow, deep kiss; a kiss that is both a claim and a reassurance. "I love when you call me baby," he murmurs against my lips.

I smirk into the kiss, the shock momentarily forgotten in the rush of his touch.

He pulls back, his eyes blazing with a fierce, terrifying determination. "I'm serious. I'll arrange it. You will be mine."

My whole body is tingling now, a dizzying mix of

excitement and disbelief. He has to be kidding, right? Because that's just insane.

Before I can process the insanity, his hands are on me, searching, claiming. The shift is immediate, a sudden, urgent need that mirrors the frantic, terrified beat of my own heart. His touch is rougher now, less tender, more primal. His fingers, thick and calloused, work the tiny, pearl buttons of my white blouse with surprising speed, then the zipper of my black slacks. The sound of the metal teeth separating is loud in the quiet room, a harsh prelude to the chaos.

He doesn't just remove the clothes; he worships the skin beneath. His lips following the path of his hands, brushing my skin as he traces the curve of my waist, the flare of my hip, the soft skin of my belly. "You're perfect," he mumbles, the words muffled against my skin, his breath hot. "And you're all mine."

He pulls back, his gaze locking with mine in a silently binding promise that is more potent than any spoken vow. "And I'm all yours, Posey. Only yours, okay?" The question is a demand, a plea for my final surrender.

I nod, a small, jerky movement. My throat is too tight for words, choked by the sheer intensity of his focus. The absolute certainty in his eyes, the dark, unwavering devotion, is the only answer I need. It is the truth I have been waiting for.

I help him, my own hands suddenly eager. I push my slacks down, letting them pool around my ankles, then quickly undo his own pants. The material parts, and his thick cock springs free, a massive, rigid length. I wrap my hand around him, my fingers barely meeting, and begin slowly pumping the hard, velvet length. The texture is like hot silk over steel.

He groans, a deep, guttural sound that vibrates in the air, his eyes closing for a brief, blissful moment of pure sensation. "I love your hand wrapped around me," he rasps, his voice thick with need. "I love the feel of you on my skin."

He pulls my blouse off my shoulders. It drops to the floor, leaving me naked save for my underwear. I quickly unbutton his top, desperate to feel the solid reality of him. My hands run over his chest, tracing the hard lines of muscle and the intricate patterns of his tattoos; each one a map of his violent life. His body is my favourite thing to touch, his skin, his strength, the beautifully dangerous canvas that is him.

I go back to his dick, my hand moving up and down his thick length, my pace quickening, driving him to the edge. He can't wait. He sinks three fingers into my wet pussy, his touch deep and demanding, finding the exact spot that makes my hips buck.

He growls, a low, feral sound that is pure, unadulterated male hunger. "Do you know every time I touch you, you're dripping, Posey? Your pussy knows you belong to me. It knows that it only wants my cock." The words are filthy, and they make me wetter, my body betraying my mind with its desperate, immediate response.

He scoops me up, my legs instinctively wrapping around his waist, and places me back against the massive glass wall. The cool glass is a shock against my heated skin, a sharp but grounding sensation. He positions his thick, hard length at my opening, slowly, and agonisingly dropping me down on his dick.

The stretch is everything; a slow, painfully exquisite fullness that makes me gasp, my head tilting back against the glass. He is massive, he is overwhelming, he is everything, and that is scary, but I know if he says we will marry, I won't stop him. Somewhere along the way, I started to love this cage he made for me, the isolation, the protection, the singular focus of his attention. And although that scares me, it also makes me feel safe. He makes me safe.

He starts to fuck me hard against the glass, the sounds of our skin slapping together and our ragged moans filling the room. He lifts and drops me on his dick over and over again, each thrust a brutal, claim that drives the air from my lungs. My head tilts back, and I look down at the floor below, the tiny figures of the gamblers blurred by the glass. I have no idea if the glass is see-through or not, if the world below is watching our desperate, public claiming; but right now, I don't care. All I care about is Catcher, and the fact that he said I was it. Only me.

I shatter around his dick, the orgasm a violently beautiful explosion that makes my body convulse, my muscles clamping down on him with desperate strength. He follows, his own release a deep, guttural roar, filling me up with his hot cum as he says, his voice a desperate rasp, "You will always be mine, Posey. Only you. There is never going to be another."

Chapter 23

Catcher

I sit in the back of the black SUV, wondering if posey is ok curled up in our bed alone. The air is thick with anticipation and the overpowering cologne Aurelio wears; he seems to think he needs the whole bottle every day. Outside the tinted window, the neon sign of a brothel flickers, a cheap, tawdry beacon in the Melbourne night.

Gabe is in the driver's seat, his face a mask of focus as he stares at the building. Aurelio is beside him, a mirror image of calm, but a dangerous, barely contained energy hums beneath the surface.

This is it. The second to last piece of the puzzle. This place is owned by the Serbians, the same bastards who used to buy women from the trafficking ring we've been dismantling. We've taken over the rest of their operations, one bloody mess at a time. Only three left now, and when this one falls; we'll own all of Melbourne. Well, bar the last two, but they are privately owned so they will be easily taken over. The thought is a cold, satisfying weight in my gut.

I know this is going to be a mess. It always is. But I don't care. The police have been paid off, the local patrol cars conveniently rerouted for the next three hours. That's our window. Three hours of controlled chaos before anyone arrives to the noise. By then, we'll be long gone, and the establishment will be ours.

Gabe raises his phone to his ear, his voice low and commanding. "Get ready," he says into the receiver, speaking to the men he has stationed around the perimeter. He ends the call, then turns to us, his eyes hard and unwavering.

"Ready?"

Aurelio and I both nod. My hand tightens around the grip of my 9mm, I love this gun, I've had her for three years now, and she has never let me down.

"I'm fucking excited," Aurelio says, his voice a low, eager purr.

Gabe rolls his eyes, a flicker of exasperation crossing his face. Aurelio might be one of my oldest friends, a man I trust with my life, but he has a funny way of looking at blood. A funny way of enjoying the violence.

I look at him. He's all clean lines and sharp edges, a black suit with the jacket discarded, the black shirt pristine. He's holding a 9mm in his hand, and there's a happy, almost beatific smile on his face. He looks like he's about to open a Christmas present, not walk into a bloodbath.

A thought, slow and heavy, occurs to me. It's a ridiculous, almost comical observation,

"A thought just occurred to me," I say, my voice cutting through the tension.

Gabe raises a brow, waiting.

"Do you have a blood kink?" I ask Aurelio, the question deadpan.

Gabe throws his head back and laughs, a loud, barking sound that is quickly muffled by the car's interior. "You only just figured that out now?"

Aurelio just smirks at me, a flash of white teeth in the gloom.

I shrug, genuinely perplexed. "Honestly, it never occurred to me. I just thought you were a messy bastard."

Gabe shakes his head, still chuckling. "You don't honestly think someone would really be covered in as much blood as he gets on himself, when we seem to get none. Far out, Catcher, you've taken too many hits to the head, mate."

They laugh at me, the sound a brief but necessary release of tension. I let them. They're right. I have taken a few too many hits to the head.

Then, Gabe's phone rings. He answers it, listens for a second, and his face snaps back to the grim mask of the enforcer.

"Time to go, boys."

The laughter dies instantly. The car doors open, and we rush from the relative safety of the SUV and into the harsh, neon-lit reality of the brothel.

The moment we burst through the door, the night explodes into chaos. The air, already stale with cheap perfume and desperation, is instantly choked with the sharp, metallic tang of gunpowder.

It is a blood bath.

The interior of the brothel is a gaudy, velvet-lined nightmare. I move on instinct. The first two guards are at the reception desk, their eyes wide with shock. My silenced 9mm spits twice, the soft thwip-thwip barely audible over the sudden, piercing screams of the women. They drop before they can even raise their own weapons.

We sweep through the ground floor. Gabe is better than he gives himself credit for, his movements economical and deadly. Aurelio, of course, is in his element, a terrifying grin plastered on his face as he dispatches a man trying to scramble out of a back room. The sound of the shots is deafening, the echoes bouncing off the mirrored walls.

The scene is a ruin. Bodies littering the plush carpet, as dark stains bloom on the cheap fabric. The air is thick with the smell of copper and fear. I kick open a door to a hallway lined with small, numbered rooms. The women are pouring out, terrified and half-dressed, their faces pale and streaked with tears.

"Out!" I roar, my voice cutting through the panic. "Waiting van! Go!"

My men, who had secured the perimeter, are already moving in, calm and professional. They herd the women, guiding them toward the back exit, and towards the waiting transport that will take them to a safe house. The screams slowly turn into whimpers, then a stunned, disbelieving silence as they realise they are being rescued, not punished.

We reach the main office, a final pocket of resistance. Gabe and I clear the room in a synchronised ballet of death. The last Serbian guard falls, his blood splattering across a framed picture of a smiling, bearded man, presumably the owner.

Just as the last of the women are being loaded, the

expected backup arrives. A black sedan screeches to a halt outside with four men piling out, weapons drawn. They are too late.

Gabe doesn't even flinch. He steps out of the doorway, his silhouette framed by the flashing neon sign. The ensuing exchange is quick, brutal, and utterly one-sided. Our men, positioned on the roof and in the adjacent alley, open fire. The carload of Serbians gunned down before they can even register the threat. The sedan is instantly riddled with holes, the windows shattering into a million glittering pieces.

We drag the last remaining man, the one who looked like the leader, back into the office. He's bleeding from a graze on his shoulder, his eyes wide with terror.

Gabe stands over him, his voice dangerously calm. "Tell your boss this: I now own this brothel. Tell him to stay away from Melbourne. If he or any of his men ever come after me, or anyone under my protection, I will kill them. Not just them. Their families. Their children. Do you understand?"

The man nods frantically, tears mixing with the blood on his face. Gabe kicks him hard in the ribs, a final, brutal punctuation mark, before signalling for him to be released. He's a message, a warning scrawled in blood.

I turn my attention to the remaining women, the ones who are too stunned or too scared to move. They huddle in a corner, their eyes darting between the bodies and us.

I step forward, lowering my voice, trying to project calm into the chaos. "Listen to me. You have three choices. One: You can go. You are free. We will give you money and transport you anywhere you want to go. Two: You can stay working here, but you will be paid an actual wage, you will be safe, and you will be treated with respect. Three: You can go and work for one of the Gallo's businesses, as maids, cleaning staff at hotels, or in one of the many restaurants he owns."

They are all shocked, not trusting. Their eyes are hollow, their minds unable to process the sudden shift from slavery to choice. But they still do as they are told, slowly beginning to move toward the men who will take them to safety.

Aurelio appears at my side. He has a few dots of blood on his face and his hands, which are covered in a thick, dark sheen. He looks like a painter who has just finished a masterpiece.

I shake my head. "I have no idea how I didn't fucking work it out sooner."

Aurelio grins, wiping a smear of blood from his cheek with the back of his hand. "You've been too pussy whipped to notice anything, brother."

I just shrug. He's not wrong. The world has been reduced to Posey, and everything else is just background noise.

"You're not wrong," I concede, looking at the ruin around us.

Chapter 24

Posey

I am bored.

The word is a small, irritating pebble under my tongue; a constant, low-grade hum of discontent that is almost worse than fear. I am lying in Catcher's massive bed, the sheets, still faintly scented with his cologne, sweat, and the ghost of our last, desperate coupling. The sheet tangled around my legs as I stare at the ceiling. The ceiling is white, unblemished, and utterly uninteresting. It's been three days since he told me he was going to marry me, three days since the dizzying, terrifying intimacy against the glass, and three days since he left for whatever dark business calls him away.

I hate when Catcher is not home. The house, usually a sanctuary, becomes a vast, silent tomb. I've trained until my muscles screamed, I've read the few books I own until the words blurred, and I've stared at the gate code on the fridge until the numbers became meaningless shapes. Now, I'm just bored.

And the boredom brings the thoughts. The dangerous, quiet thoughts.

There is something profoundly, fundamentally wrong with me. He said he would marry me, and I am not opposed to the idea. I am not running. I never truly fought to get out of this place, and I am not about to start now. The cage door is open, and I am choosing to stay inside. The thought is a confession, a surrender.

Maybe growing up the way I had, means I grew up broken? A piece of me, the part that should scream for freedom, is missing, replaced by a strange, desperate need for his protection. He is the darkness I crave, the violence that makes me feel safe. He is the only constant, the only certainty.

"Fuck," I hiss, the sound barely a whisper, as I roll over and punch the pillow. I try to force myself back to sleep, to escape the relentless loop of my own introspection. It's impossible, and it's annoying.

Then, a sound.

A small, almost imperceptible beep. A tiny, electronic death knell that cuts through the silence like a razor.

I sit up instantly, my fighter's instincts snapping me to full alert. I look at the clock that sits on Catcher's bedside table. It's one of those digital ones you plug into the wall socket, a simple, functional thing.

It's off.

The screen is blank, dark. Did the house lose power? I reach out and turn the lamp on the bedside table. Nothing. The room remains plunged in the deep, suffocating darkness of night. The silence now absolute; like an unnaturally heavy blanket.

What the hell.

Then I hear it. A noise from downstairs. It's not the wind, not the house settling. It's a distinct, heavy footstep. A deliberately measured weight on the tile.

My heart slams against my ribs, a frantic, trapped bird. Who the fuck is that? The gate, the alarms, the perimeter sensors, Catcher's security is a fortress. No way someone got in…

What the fuck is happening?

Is it Catcher? It can't be. He would call out. He would announce his presence. He would never sneak into his own house like this.

And this is more than one voice. I can hear a low, muffled conversation rising from the ground floor. A harsh, rhythmic murmur.

I slide out of the bed, my bare feet silent on the floor as I creep to the door of Catcher's room; my body low and tight, ready to move. I press myself against the wall, hiding behind the door, my breath held tight in my chest.

The voices get closer and closer, the footsteps heavier, more deliberate. They are coming up the stairs.

I can't understand the language, though. It's not English. It's a harsh, guttural sound, a foreign tongue that sends a cold spike of terror straight through me.

I press my back flat against the wall behind the door, forcing myself to slow my breathing. I try to get my heart to stop beating so loud, but it's a frantic drum against my ribs, so loud I can hear it in my own ears. Every thump is a betrayal, a beacon to the men downstairs.

I stare from where I'm hiding, my eyes darting around the room. My gaze lands on the mobile phone Catcher gave me that sits the bedside table. I nearly swear out loud. *Fuck.* I should have grabbed it. I should have called him.

But I've lived my whole life without one, my father seeing no use for one for me. Catcher has been teaching me how to use it for three days now, but it's still a strange contraption, a symbol of a world I don't fully grasp. I should have grabbed it and called him. *Fuck,* I think again, the word a silent scream of frustration.

The voices get closer. They are slowing, methodically checking all the rooms. I can hear the doors opening and closing, the heavy thud of their boots on the wooden floor, the low, foreign chatter. They are getting closer and closer to the room.

I brace myself. I have two choices: I'll either make a run for it, or I'll fight. My hands clench into fists, my body tightening into a coiled spring.

Finally, they get to Catcher's room. The door handle turns, and they enter. I'm still concealed behind the door, pretty much holding my breath.

Then, one of them speaks, and the language shifts.

"She was here. Where the fuck is she now?"

They know I was here. They are looking for me.

They start to check the room. I spread my legs a little more silently, shifting my weight, getting ready to pounce. I'll have to fight, then run.

The door is pulled back.

I'm staring into the face of the man who was yelling at Milan the other week in the ring. The one that looked the same as Milan.

What the fuck, I think, the shock momentarily freezing me.

But only for a second. My training takes over. I spring out from behind the door and punch him right in the throat. It's a clean hit; a brutally focused strike.

He doubles over, a strangled, gurgling sound escaping his lips, leaving me enough room to quickly run past.

I don't make it far. I am scooped up into the arms of the other massive, immovable wall of muscle. I swing my elbow to the left and up, and it connects with something hard, his jaw, his temple, I don't know.

He grunts, a sharp, surprised sound, before letting go of me.

I scramble away, out of the room, down the stairs, my bare feet slapping against them, the sound a frantic drumbeat in the sudden silence. I run for the front door, my hand reaching for the handle, a desperate hope surging through me.

It's locked.

Or worse, it's turned off. I try the handle, twisting it with all my strength, but it won't move. It's dead, sealed shut. What the fuck? The security system must be down, locking everything in place.

I pivot instantly, my mind racing, and run for the back door. The one Catcher and I use to go out to the porch. I try the handle. It opens. Thank God.

I burst out onto the porch, the cool night air a shock against my skin. I don't stop to think, just run, leaping off the steps and onto the dry, cracked earth. I run for the gate, the only way out, the symbol of my freedom.

I am muttering the code over and over, a frantic, desperate prayer: "Two-two-eight-four-three-seven." I reach the keypad, my fingers shaking, and punch in the numbers.

Nothing.

No beep. No click. Not even the faint glow of the screen. Fuck. The power is out. The gate is dead.

I hear them now. The heavy, running footsteps of the men chasing me. I turn and see them, two dark shapes emerging from the shadow of the house. It's nighttime, so it's dark, and I can hardly see, but the shapes are getting closer to me, too close.

My hand reaches out to touch the fence. It's a massive, high chain-link barrier, topped with razor wire. It's normally electric and zaps anything that touches it.

Nothing.

It's cold, inert metal. Fuck, I think, the realisation a cold, hard knot in my stomach. The power was disconnected on purpose. This wasn't a random break-in. This was planned.

I run along the fence line, my eyes frantically scanning the dark metal. They had to have gotten in somehow. They had to have climbed it or cut a hole, right?

I hear their voices again, closer now, swallowed by the vastness of the bush, their foreign language a harsh, angry bark.

Then I find it. A section of the fence, near the ground, has been cut and bent back, a jagged, dark opening just big enough for a person to squeeze through.

Just as their voices get closer, I drop to my belly and push myself through the hole. The sharp, torn metal tears at my skin, biting and cutting it, but I don't feel the pain. I push through, scrambling to my feet on the other side.

I run. I run right into the bush as fast as I can. The dense, dark Australian scrub is a terrifying, unfamiliar labyrinth, but it's my only chance. Tree branches slap me in the face, stinging my eyes. I trip on things on the ground, unseen roots and rocks, but I get up and keep running.

The darkness here is absolute, a suffocating black velvet that swallows the distant, angry shouts of the men. The air is no longer cool and clean; it's thick with the cloying, medicinal scent of eucalyptus and the dry, dusty smell of the earth. Every step is a gamble. My bare feet, already cut by the ground, now land on sharp, unseen stones and brittle twigs that snap like tiny gunshots under my weight.

The bush is alive.

The silence of the house is replaced by a cacophony of alien sounds. The screech of a possum overhead sounds like a woman being murdered. The rustle of a snake, or maybe just a lizard, in the dry leaves beside me sends a jolt of pure, paralysing terror through my spine. I can hear the chirp of unseen insects; a thousand tiny, clicking noises that amplify the feeling of being watched.

I am more scared out here in the bush than I was in the house. In the house, the threat was human, a known quantity. Here, the threat is primal, ancient, and everywhere. I can fight a man. I can't fight the darkness, the venom, the endless, indifferent wilderness.

I have to find somewhere safe. The voices of the men are distant now, swallowed by the vastness of the bush, but I don't stop. I don't dare. I push deeper, letting the branches tear at my skin, the pain a welcome distraction from the cold, deep fear.

I run until my lungs burn, until the air I drag in feels like fire, until my legs ache with a dull, throbbing agony. I run until the only sound is the frantic, desperate pounding of my own heart, a rhythm that is slowly and terrifyingly being absorbed by the wild, indifferent heart of the bush. I run until I collapse, gasping, my body shaking not just from exertion, but from the raw, unadulterated terror of being utterly alone in the dark.

Chapter 25

Catcher

I slam the rear door of the van shut. The heavy metal thud echoing in the alley, a final, ugly punctuation mark on the night's violence. The last of the pale and wide-eyed girls are safely loaded, headed for a temporary safe house Gabe set up. I watch the van pull away, the taillights disappearing into the city's grime. A flicker of something close to pride warms the cold knot in my chest, but it's quickly replaced by the lingering stench of this place; a concoction of cheap perfume, stale smoke, and the metallic tang of fresh blood. My men are already moving through the brothel, cleaning up the mess and securing the property. We are turning this into something that won't make me sick to look at. I hope the women realise they have a choice here. A real one. I hope they take it. The thought of Posey, safe at home, is the only thing that keeps me grounded in this filth. She is the clean slate, the reason for all this brutal effort.

I turn to Gabe. He's already on his phone, barking orders to the cleanup crew. His low, controlled rumble is the sound of authority, a familiar comfort. "That's it. Let's get out of here before the cops decide it's time to show up." The window of opportunity is closing, and I don't want to be here when the official cleanup starts.

Aurelio is beside me, his face dotted with blood; his hands covered in it. He grins, as he rubs them together, making the blood start to congeal. His eyes, usually so sharp, hold a manic gleam. "Best Tuesday night in months, brother." He's a monster, but he's our monster.

My phone chooses that moment to ping in my pocket. It's not a call or a text. It's a security alert. A single, chilling vibration that cuts through the post-battle adrenaline. I pull it out, frowning.

MAIN POWER OFFLINE.

The words flash red against the screen. A cold dread settling in my gut. I pull up the grid I have on my phone, a proprietary system that monitors my entire property. The screen is a sea of red. All main power is out, the gate, the perimeter fence, the house's primary system. Everything. The fortress is blind.

Except for the cameras. They run off a dedicated, battery and system backup. The only thing still breathing in my fortress.

I tap the screen, bringing up the live feed. The image is grainy, black-and-white, but clear enough. I watch with complete disbelief as two men start cutting through my fence. They are working with a speed that speaks of planning.

"FUCK!" I roar, the sound ripping from my throat. I

don't wait to see them climb under. I don't wait for the next frame.

I start running to the SUV, already yelling. "Gabe! Aurelio! Get the fuck in the car now!"

Gabe shoves his phone in his pocket, his eyes wide at the raw panic in my voice. Aurelio doesn't even hesitate, dropping his 9mm into its holster. They both run and dive into the SUV, no questions asked, just the instinct of men who know when the game has changed.

I slide into the driver's seat, the leather cold against my back, and slam the door. The engine roars to life, a desperate, hungry sound. I don't bother with the seatbelt. I punch the accelerator, the tires screaming as the SUV fishtails out of the alley and onto the main road.

"What the fuck happened?" Gabe finally demands, his voice tight with adrenaline.

I don't look at him. My eyes are glued to the road, the city lights blurring into streaks of red and white. "Power's out. Two men are cutting through the fence. They're in my house."

"Who?" Aurelio asks, his voice suddenly cold, all the humour gone.

"I don't know," I say, my jaw clenching.

The house is an hour away from where we are. I push the SUV past any reasonable speed limit, the speedometer needle climbing higher and higher. Every second is a lifetime. I had given her the code. I had given her the choice. And now, someone else is trying to take her.

No one touches what is mine.

I grip the steering wheel, the leather groaning under the pressure.

I shove the phone at Gabe, not taking my eyes off the road. "Give me a play by play."

Gabe catches the phone one-handed, his fingers immediately flying across the screen, expertly manipulating the proprietary system. He brings up the camera feeds, switching angles, his eyes scanning the grainy, black-and-white images.

"Found them," he mutters, his voice low and focused. "They are climbing the stairs."

My knuckles go white on the wheel, the leather digging into my palms. I can feel the tension radiating off Aurelio and Gabe. The silence in the car is a suffocating thing, broken only by the roar of the engine.

Gabe goes quiet for a beat, his breath held tight. Then, a sharp exhale. "She is running down the stairs."

My breath catches in my throat. I don't realise I am speaking until the words are out, a desperate, raw whisper. "Run, little bird. Fucking run."

Gabe keeps his eyes glued to the phone, pressing screen by screen, watching my woman run for her life. My heart is in my throat, a frantic, painful thing. I am panicking, a feeling I haven't allowed myself to feel since I was a kid.

"Fuck," Gabe spits. "The front door won't open."

I swear, a low, guttural sound. "It runs off the main system. It will be locked with no power. The back door should open though. Fuck, baby, run for that."

"She is," Gabe confirms, his voice strained. "She is running for the back door now. She is outside and heading for the gate."

"Fuck, it's not gonna open either..." I slam my fist

against the steering wheel, the pain barely registering. "So much for having the code. It won't fucking work right now."

Gabe's voice is a mix of awe and terror. "She is running along the fence now. Fuck, she runs fast, Catcher. She might be okay..."

Aurelio, who has been leaning over the seat to watch the phone with Gabe, reaches out. His hand rests on my shoulder, squeezing hard. "She is slipping under the hole they made. She is running, mate. Fucking running for the bush. They are only now just getting under the fence. Fuck..."

I push the accelerator to the floor. The SUV surges forward, the engine screaming a desperate, echoing promise. I'm coming, Posey. Hold on.

Gabe settles back in his seat, the car going silent now. They can't see anything. The last image was a grainy shot of the two men disappearing into the blackness of the scrub. Posey is gone.

I feel sick. The adrenaline is curdling into a cold, murderous rage. I am going to kill those men. I am going to rip the heads off their bodies.

Aurelio breaks the silence, his voice low and thoughtful. "The bald guy looked a lot like the guy you fought a few weeks back."

Gabe frowns. "He did, actually. Maybe it's the one who yelled at the fighter."

"I don't fucking care who it was," I growl, my voice a low, dangerous rumble. "They are dead." And I mean it. They are dead no matter what.

"True that, mate," Gabe says, his voice calm, a deliberate attempt to ground me. "We're only ten minutes away now."

The dark country road is empty. We haven't passed a single car, which is a blessing and a curse. No witnesses but makes me wonder how the men got down to my property.

I come screeching to a stop out the front of my house, the SUV kicking up a cloud of dust and gravel. I don't wait for the engine to die. I rip the door open and race from the car, heading straight for the fence line, Gabe and Aurelio right behind me.

I rip the gun from my holster and click off the safety. I don't bother with the hole in the fence; I vault over the hood of the SUV and plunge into the bush.

"Posey!" I start calling her name, over and over, my voice sounding frantic, scared.

The wildlife is getting thicker, the animal noises louder as I get further in. The sounds of the bush are a thousand tiny, mocking echoes.

"Posey!"

Until I hear a small voice, faint and choked with sobs. "Catcher?"

I look to the left, then the right, my heart hammering against my ribs. "Little bird, where are you?"

She speaks again; this time it's from my right. I turn, Gabe and Aurelio sliding to a stop behind me, their guns drawn, scanning the darkness.

"Posey?"

"I'm here..."

I follow her voice to a big, thick bush on the ground. I crouch down, my gun still raised, and see a small, shivering shape curled up beneath the dense foliage. "You there, little bird?"

She sobs. I reach in and pull her out.

So much relief rushes through me, a tidal wave that nearly buckles my knees. She is a mess. Tears are running down her face, small cuts on her face and arms from running in only her sleep shorts and singlet. She is shivering, her teeth chattering.

I drop my gun. It hits the dirt with a dull thud. I scoop her into my arms, holding her close to my chest, burying my face in her hair. She really sobs now, clinging to me, her body shaking violently.

"It's okay, baby. I got you, okay? It's okay. You're safe." I hold her tighter, my voice a gentle, fierce whisper. "I'm going to fucking kill those men, baby. It's okay."

She sobs and says, her voice muffled against my chest, "It was the guys from the fight. The one yelling at Milan."

Aurelio steps forward, his face grim. "I fucking thought so."

Chapter 26

Posey

Catcher shoves me into the back of the SUV. The force of it, though not malicious, is a shock that rattles my teeth. The door slams shut, the heavy metal thud a final, brutal sound that seals me back into the safety of a metal cage. I land awkwardly on the leather seat next to Aurelio, who climbed into the other side just as quickly as Catcher shoved me in. My body is a landscape of aches and stinging cuts, but the immediate and paralysing fear is beginning to recede, replaced by a cold, clinical awareness.

Aurelio's hands, I notice immediately, are covered in dried, cracked blood. The sight should repulse me, should send me scrambling to the opposite side of the seat, but it doesn't. The scent of it, coppery and stale, mixes with the rich leather and the lingering smell of too much cologne. It's a scent of violence, yes, but also of protection.

I am not crying anymore. The tears stopped on the walk back to the SUV, not because the fear was gone, but because my body had simply run out of fluid. Catcher carried me the whole way, my body a dead weight against his chest, his frantic energy a shield against the cold night. The memory of his arms around me, the sheer, raw panic in his voice when he found me, is a warmth that is slowly chasing the hypothermia from my bones. He was terrified. He was terrified for me. That single, undeniable truth is a powerful anchor.

Now, he's gone, heading into the house with Gabe, guns drawn, to check for any remaining threat. I watch the two dark shapes disappear into the blackness, and a wave of fresh, cold terror washes over me. I am alone again, but not truly alone.

Aurelio sits next to me, his own gun ready in his blood covered hands. He catches my eye, and I raise my brows at him, a silent question that hangs heavy in the air. The man is a killer, a fact that should terrify me, but right now, he is a familiar, predictable threat; a solid wall of protection.

"Fun night?" I ask, my voice surprisingly steady, though it feels like it belongs to someone else. The words are a defence mechanism, a way to prove I haven't completely shattered.

His face splits into a wide, unsettling smile, a flash of white in the darkness. "Well, yes, it was. Thank you for asking."

I shake my head at him, a small, weary movement. "You have a thing for blood."

He raises his own brows at me, a flicker of genuine surprise in his eyes. "You worked that out a lot quicker than Catcher."

"Not hard to work out," I say, the words coming out with a dry, observational tone. My mind, which had been a frantic mess of survival, is now settling into its old pattern: observation. It's the only tool I've ever truly possessed. "Most people would have wiped their hands to clear it off, instead of leaving it there, making it hard to grip your gun with wet, slippery hands."

Aurelio chuckles, a deep, rumbling sound that vibrates through the seat. "You see a lot more than you let on, don't you, *little bird?*" He says the ending like a joke, but his eyes are sharp, assessing, and I know he sees the truth in my statement.

"I'm used to being seen, not heard," I say, the old, familiar truth slipping out. "So it's not hard to see a lot when you're only allowed to observe." It's a strange comfort, this shared moment of dark understanding with a man whose hands are covered in cracked blood. I feel safe. Safer than I have ever felt in my life, surrounded by these three men who are capable of such violence. They are my shield, my wall, my cage.

Aurelio nods slowly, the humour fading, replaced by a thoughtful seriousness. "I like you, Posey."

"I'm not sure if I'm flattered or scared," I admit, and he laughs again, a genuine, full-bodied sound that breaks the tension.

The passenger and driver side doors open, Catcher and Gabe climb in, each holding a stuffed duffle bag. Catcher's eyes are wild, a little red around the sides. He was truly terrified. The raw, unmasked fear I saw in his face when he found me is a more potent declaration of love than any words. It makes me realise he isn't lying when he says he wants me. He was afraid to lose me.

"What the fuck is so funny?" Catcher demands, his voice rough with adrenaline and residual fear, as he turns and looks back at me.

I lean forward, my hand resting on his face, my thumb gently tracing the sharp line of his jaw. "Your friend has a blood kink."

Catcher frowns, then runs a hand over his own head. "Fuck. I *have* taken too many hits to the head."

Gabe laughs, and so does Aurelio. I frown, genuinely confused. "I don't understand."

"I only worked it out tonight," Catcher says, shaking his head in disbelief.

"Really?" I ask, the disbelief clear in my voice.

"Yep."

I smile at him, a small but genuine smile, and he smiles back, the wildness in his eyes softening just for me. "I thought I lost you, baby. You okay?"

"I'll be fine," I say, the words a promise to him and myself. The cuts on my arms sting, my muscles ache, and the memory of the man's face is burned into my mind, but I am alive. I am safe. "Where are we going?"

Gabe answers from the driver's seat. "My house. You can't go back there now."

I frown. "Why?"

Catcher takes my hand, his grip tight and reassuring. "No one is meant to know where I live, we'll need to move. I own a few more properties, but they are not hooked up like this one. So, we will stay at Gabe's till we have one hooked up."

I nod, the logic of their dark world making perfect sense. My fear is still a cold, heavy weight, but it is now manageable and contained.

The drive to Gabe's house takes a tense, silent forty-five minutes. I watch the landscape change from the dense, dark bush to the manicured, wealthy suburbs. I notice that Gabe's place is not the sprawling, fortress-like compound I had imagined for the leader of a mafia-like organisation. It's big, certainly, a modern, two-story structure of glass and rendered brick, but it lacks the imposing, isolated might of Catcher's home.

But then I see the guards. They line the property, spaced out but visible, their presence a silent, undeniable warning. They are easy to spot, probably on purpose, so anyone who tries to break in knows fully well that no one can. This isn't a fortress; it's a statement.

Gabe presses a control on his visor, and the gate slides open, revealing a long, winding driveway. We drive in, and the SUV pulls up to the front door. A massive guard in a crisp suit, opens the door for Gabe, letting him out. Gabe talks to him in low, quick tones, his face serious.

Catcher gets out next, then opens my door. I climb out into his waiting arms, the cold night air hitting my exposed skin. I place a hand over his chest; his heart is still beating a little bit fast, a frantic rhythm that mirrors the fear still thrumming in my own veins.

"You okay, baby?" I ask, the question a reflex, a need to check on the man who just saved me.

He wraps his arms around me tightly, pulling me into his chest. "No," he says, the word a raw, honest whisper against my hair.

I lay my head on his chest, wrapping my arms around him too. We just stand like that for a bit, two broken pieces fitting back together. The world can wait.

"It's alright, I'll carry your bags for you," Aurelio says, walking past us, a duffle bag slung over each shoulder.

"You would make a good bell boy, you know that," Catcher says, his voice muffled against my hair, a small, genuine laugh escaping him.

Aurelio laughs back. "Fuck off."

Catcher steals me into the house. The door is held open by a woman who is standing and waiting. I watch as Gabe leans down, kissing her deeply; a long possessive kiss that speaks volumes. Then he walks in. Aurelio walks past her, not touching her at all, ensuring a respectful distance is maintained.

She keeps holding the door, waiting for us. She is short and has the brightest red hair I have ever seen. It's not a dark, auburn red either; it's a bright, almost orange colour, and it looks amazing against her pale, freckle-dotted skin. This must be Alba, Gabe's wife. She is fucking stunning and has the greenest eyes I have ever seen.

As we walk in, Alba's eyes trace my body, taking in the cuts, the dirt, the tear tracks on my face. She doesn't flinch.

"I'll go grab the first aid kit," she says, her voice soft but firm. "We need to clean those cuts." And she takes off, disappearing down a hallway.

The house is stunning inside. All white walls and clean line furniture. But there are a few homely touches everywhere, like fresh flowers, throw pillows, and blankets. Photos litter the walls, of her and Gabe. Some look old, from when they were a lot younger, then heaps from recently. No wedding photos, though, and it makes me rethink; I swear Catcher said wife.

Catcher leads me to a stool where he makes me sit, then he starts to look at my cuts, his touch feather-light, his face a mask of concern.

Alba returns, placing her hands on her hips, a small, no-nonsense figure. "Okay, you need to come with me. We need to clean this all up."

Catcher goes to walk with us, but Alba holds her hand up. "Nope. You stay."

He frowns, his possessive instinct kicking in. She stares him down, her green eyes unwavering. "No. Stay."

He puffs up, ready to argue, but Alba points at the loungeroom behind him. "Go now, Catcher."

He deflates, the exhaustion and adrenaline finally winning. He gives me one last, desperate look, then goes.

Alba leads me down a short, brightly lit hallway and into a small spare room. It's simple, clean, and quiet, containing only a large, inviting bed and a bathroom attached.

She turns to me, her green eyes softening with genuine concern. "Are you okay?"

I smile and nod, a little uneasy. I'm not used to this kind of gentle attention from a woman, especially one who just bossed Catcher around.

"Okay," she says, accepting the answer without pushing. "Get in that shower. I'll go and grab you some clothes to put on. Aurelio had duffle bags, I'm assuming they are yours?"

I nod again, grateful for her efficiency. I head into the

bathroom and close the door. I look at my reflection in the mirror; I'm a wild-eyed, dirt-streaked creature with leaves still tangled in her hair. I would rather Catcher was with me, his presence is a solid comfort, but I'm not going to fight this. Alba is right; I need to be clean.

I undress, my clothes falling to the floor in a pile of torn, filthy fabric. I climb into the shower and turn the water on, letting the hot spray hit my skin. It stings. Every single small cut on my body, from the fence and the bush, screams in protest. My feet are the worst, the soles tender and raw, stinging with each step I take to turn under the water.

But I wash the dirt from my body, scrubbing the grime from my skin. I watch the water turn brown, then black, as it goes down the drain, carrying away the fear and the filth of the night. I even give my hair a quick wash with some of the shampoo and conditioner I find in the shower.

I'm actually shocked at the amount of sticks and leaves all washing off of me, swirling down the drain. I must have looked like a feral animal.

A small, gentle knock comes on the door. "It's just me," Alba says softly. "I'm putting the clothes down on the bench." The door opens a crack, then closes again.

I turn the water off and step out, grabbing the soft, fluffy towel. Drying my body hurts with each swipe of the towel; the friction a painful reminder of my escape. I quickly get dressed into the clothes Alba left: a soft pair of shorts and a t-shirt. They smell like Catcher, a clean, familiar scent that makes my eyes prickle with fresh tears of relief. I am safe. I am clean. And I am here.

I open the door and step back into the room and see

Alba there with the first aid spread out. She gestures to the bed. "Sit."

I do.

Alba gets to work cleaning my cuts with a brown liquid. It stings each time she dabs it on a cut, and I hiss, pulling my arm back instinctively. Alba talks as she goes, gentle words that are a balm to my frayed nerves. "It's very nice to finally meet you, Posey. I have no idea what happened, but I'm assuming it wasn't fun. Gabe not messaging me in advance means it was something fast, and he had no chance to say anything."

I find myself responding, short sentences at first, but responding, nonetheless. The sweet, gentle words are pulling the truth from me, not poking and prodding, but coaxing. "People broke into Catcher's house. They tried to attack me. I managed to run out of the house and into the bush."

Alba listens, her green eyes focused on my skin, her brow furrowed in concentration. "Oh, Posey," she answers so sweetly, her voice full of genuine sympathy. I watch her hands as they dab, careful and precise. It's then I notice the small scars that litter her own skin, tiny but there, faint white lines against her pale skin. I don't comment on it, but Catcher's words about her being stuck in the sex traffic world spin in my head.

That could have been me if Catcher hadn't saved me.

The realisation hitting hard; a cold, sickening punch to the gut, making fresh tears prickle my eyes.

Alba's green eyes stare into mine, seeing the sudden shift in my expression. "Once we are finished here, we can go back out to the men. I'm sure they are only sitting out there talking about how to murder the men who broke in anyway." She pauses, then adds with a wry smile, "Which, honestly, I do not want to hear or be a part of."

I smile at her. She is nice. Genuinely nice. And I like her. I've never had a friend. I wonder if one day she might be mine.

Chapter 27

Catcher

I sit in the lounge room, the plush white sofa making me feel uncomfortable and dirty. The exhaustion is a dull but heavy ache that settles deep in my bones, but the rage is a sharp, clean fire that keeps me from sinking. I can't rest. Not until this is handled. Not until the men who touched her are nothing but a memory.

Aurelio is on the couch opposite me, a wet wipe in his hand as he meticulously removes the last small specks of dried blood from his face. He's clean now, but the intensity in his eyes hasn't faded. He's a coiled spring, a predator waiting for the hunt to begin, and I know he's enjoying every second of this dark anticipation.

Gabe is next to me, his laptop open, the screen displaying a grainy, timestamped feed from the fight club's exterior cameras. We don't have cameras inside the club; we don't want evidence on ourselves being leaked. But we have them outside, to see who comes in and out. It's a necessary compromise in our line of work, a small window of vulnerability we allow for security.

Gabe scrolls through the footage from the night I fought Milan. The silence in the room is heavy, broken only by the soft click of the laptop keys and the faint, rhythmic sound of Aurelio wiping his skin. I watch the screen, my jaw tight, my focus absolute. Every second that passes is a second that man is still breathing, still walking free. And that thought is a poison in my blood.

Then, there he is. The angry man. The one who was yelling at Milan. He walks in, his face a mask of rage, and walks out later, his shoulders hunched in defeat. The camera catches him perfectly, a clear, damning image.

"There," Gabe says, his finger tapping the screen, freezing the frame on the man's face. "That's the one Posey recognised. The one who was yelling at Milan."

Gabe doesn't hesitate. He picks up his phone and makes a quick call to Angel in Sydney. Angel is a ghost, a digital phantom and the best in the business for this kind of thing, the absolute best. Only Matteo's son, Niko, is better; but Niko is off limits at nighttime, kids got schoolwork to do. Angel can take a single, low-resolution image and pull a full life history from the ether.

"Angel, it's Gabe. I need a favour, mate. A fast one. This is Catcher's girl. No messing around."

I can hear the muffled, groggy voice on the other end. "Gabe? It's three in the morning, you bastard. What is it?" The irritation is clear, but the underlying loyalty is stronger.

"I need a facial recon on a guy from a security feed. I'm sending you a still now. It's urgent. He broke into Catcher's place. Tried to take his women."

A sharp, female voice whines in the background,

followed by a loud, annoyed sigh. The sound of a woman being woken up by our world.

"Hold on," Angel mutters. Then, his voice sharpens, laced with irritation. "Shut up, Candy. I'll be back soon."

Aurelio leans forward, a wicked grin spreading across his face. "Ohhh, we should have FaceTimed. I wanna see what she looks like."

Angel's voice, now back on the line, is dry. "I'll send her your way, Aurelio. She ain't cheap, but she's good."

Gabe chuckles, a low, dark sound. "Focus, Angel. This is serious. I need a name, an address, and a family tree. Everything."

"I know, I know. Send me the image now. Give me a minute to pull up the software. I'll run a deep scan, cross-referencing against police databases, social media, and a few private networks I have access to." We listen as Angel pulls up his laptop and starts a search. The silence returns, thick with anticipation.

"It can take a while," Angel explains. "I'm running it against a few private databases. Want me to call you back when it's done?"

Gabe glances at me, then back at the phone. "Appreciate it, mate. Yeah, call me back."

He hangs up, and the room falls silent again. The tension a solid thing, like a coil wound too tight, ready to snap.

I run a hand down my face, the stubble rough against my palm. "I'm going to kill them both." The words are not a threat; they are a promise, a cold, hard fact that settles the frantic beating of my heart.

Gabe leans back, his expression calm. "We will help, mate. Just relax."

I huff, the sound humourless. Relax. Right.

Aurelio settles back into the couch, his eyes still sharp. "I never thought I would see the day Catcher Calcone settled down, let alone became so pussy whipped he can't function right." The banter is a necessary release, a way to bleed off the pressure.

I shrug, a small, weary movement. "Neither did I. But fuck me, I took one look at her and just knew she was mine."

Gabe nods, a knowing look in his eyes. He understands. He met Alba in primary school and has been chasing her skirt ever since. Even when she went missing, he was a mess for years. He knows what it is to be utterly consumed by one woman.

It's then that Posey and Alba reappear from the hallway.

Posey is now in a pair of shorts and one of my t-shirts. The shirt swamps her frame, hanging off her shoulders, but she has never looked sexier to me. The sight of her, clean and safe, is a punch of relief that nearly buckles my knees. It's the only thing that matters.

I instantly stand and hold my arms out. She comes straight away, a small, desperate sound escaping her as she wraps herself into my body. I wrap her up in my arms, pulling her tight against my chest. I run my hand down her wet hair.

"You okay, little bird?" I ask, my voice rough, as I watch Alba walk away into the kitchen.

She nods against my chest. "Alba cleaned all the cuts. My feet still hurt like crazy, though."

I let her go just long enough to scoop her up, so she is off her feet, then sit back on the couch with her in my arms. She is light, fragile, and utterly mine.

Gabe leans forward a little, his voice gentle. "Posey, can you tell us what happened exactly?"

She sighs, a small, tired sound, and turns to get a comfortable position in my lap.

I growl, a low warning. "Stop wiggling so much."

She blushes, a beautiful pink rising on her cheeks, and settles back, her movement stilling. My dick is already hard under her, it's like he knows her ass is near, and wants in now. The sheer audacity of my body to react like this, even now, is a testament to how deeply she affects me.

She starts to explain the whole thing to them. The power going out, the footsteps, the foreign language, the moment of recognition, the fight, the run. Every word is a fresh stab of fear, a reminder of how close I came to losing her. I hold her tighter, my jaw clenched, listening to my little bird recount her terrifying flight.

Gabe explains to her, "We have someone running facial recon on him, Posey. We'll know who he is soon."

I interject, my voice low and firm. "And I'm going to kill him."

Posey shifts in my lap, looking up at me, her eyes wide but steady. "I think I will feel safer knowing he can't come back ever again." The coldness of her agreement sends a thrill through me. She is learning my world.

I beam at her. Fuck, I love this woman. Actually, fucking love her. Not that I've told her yet, but I will one day. I already have the marriage paperwork filled out, and ready to go. I will have her as my wife.

Alba walks in from the kitchen, a small, graceful figure. She places a bottle of whiskey on the coffee table with some glasses, and a plate of biscotti. She goes to sit on the arm of the couch next to Gabe, who just scoops her off the arm and right into his lap.

"Can I have one of those whiskeys?" Gabe asks, his eyes glued to her ass as she leans forward to pour him one.

She settles back into his lap, his hand resting on her lower belly. "Thank you," he says to her, his voice thick with appreciation.

Then Gabe's phone rings. He answers it, putting it on loudspeaker.

Angel's voice comes through, no longer groggy, but sharp and professional. "Well, I got an answer quickly. The guy has a record. He's Serbian. Name is Dragon Petrovic, but they call him Crusher. He is Leon Alexander's right-hand man. He has a twin brother called Milan."

Gabe shakes his head. "I thought he looked familiar, but I wasn't able to place him."

Aurelio swears. "Fuck! No wonder he hates you, Catcher."

Chapter 28

Posey

We are back in the room that Alba cleaned me up in. It's a simple space for a guest room, but it feels like the safest place on earth. I am curled into Catcher, his arms wrapped around me so tightly I can barely draw a full breath, but I can't complain. The pressure is a comfort, a barrier against the terror that still tries to claw its way back into my mind. I can feel the phantom sting of the bushes on my skin, hear the echo of the men's footsteps, but his embrace is like a solid, unmoving shield.

His heart pounds a heavy, reassuring rhythm beneath my ear. It's a frantic beat, a sound that tells me more than any words could about the fear he felt.

"I was scared," he murmurs, his voice thick and low as they vibrate through my skull. "I thought I would lose you, Posey."

I snuggle closer, pressing my cheek against the damp cotton of his shirt. "I'm okay. I'm here."

"I know, but fuck. I've not felt fear like that since my

mum died, Posey. I was scared." The admission is raw, a crack in the impenetrable armour he usually wears. It's terrifying and beautiful all at once, a glimpse into his vulnerability.

I push myself up, leaning on my elbow so I can look into his dark pools. They are still shadowed with the remnants of panic, but they are focused entirely on me. "I'm here, Catcher."

He frames my face with his hands, his thumbs gently stroking my cheekbones. His gaze is intense and searching, as if he's trying to memorise every detail of my face; to prove I'm real and whole.

"I love you, Posey."

The words freeze every muscle in my body. The world narrows to the space between us, the air thick with the unspoken weight of that confession. It's not a question, not a demand, but a simple, profound statement of fact that shatters the last of my defences.

"Really?" I whisper, the sound barely audible.

"Yes, Posey. I love you. You're mine, little bird. I won't ever let you go."

A wave of pure, unadulterated happiness washes over me, so potent it makes my eyes sting. I smile, a genuine, unforced smile that reaches every part of my exhausted body. I lean down to kiss him, a soft, reverent press of my lips against his.

"I love you too," I whisper against his mouth. "You're my safe space. I don't think I've ever felt safe in my life until you, Catcher."

We kiss again, deeply this time, a long, slow exploration that seals the promise. His hands roam, familiar, tracing the curve of my waist, the line of my hip. But they stop. He doesn't push, doesn't demand. He just holds me, his body a warm, heavy anchor in the dark.

I run my hands under his shirt, so I can feel his skin. My fingers find the ridges of his abs, tracing the lines of muscle as we settle there. The room is quiet, the world outside a distant, muffled hum.

"Where will we live now?" I ask, the question quiet; almost getting lost in the space between us.

Catcher shifts, pulling me closer. "You can choose, if you would like. I have a few places we can go."

"Where are they?" The idea of choosing, of having a say in where my life will be, is a strange, heady feeling. It's a freedom I've never known.

Catcher leans over and grabs his phone from the bedside table, then settles back into the bed, propping himself up slightly. He types a few things into the search bar, pulling up a property website. The listings all come up marked 'Sold,' but I know why. He owns them.

He shows me the first one: an apartment in the city, overlooking the main strip, all glittery lights and towering glass. It's a penthouse, clearly; with a view that could swallow the horizon. It looks nice, expensive, a cage of gold and steel, but I grimace slightly. "It's nice…"

Catcher chuckles lightly, a deep rumble in his chest. "You can be honest, Posey. We will go where you choose."

He shows me a small house in the suburbs next, neat and tidy, a brick veneer with a manicured lawn. It's utterly normal, and that's what makes it feel wrong. Too exposed, too easy to walk up to. It doesn't look or feel right.

Then, he shows me a massive place, a sprawling estate

in what looks like the same town as Gabe. The photos show a modern, low-slung house of dark wood and glass, set back from a long, winding driveway.

"This is here? In this town?" I ask, pointing at the screen.

"Yes, about five streets away from here. It's big and has a small amount of land that surrounds it. About ten acres of cleared land, and then it backs onto a nature reserve." It's in a suburb again, but it has a fence around the whole thing, a high, black, electric fence that looks less like a decoration and more like a serious deterrent. It's impressive, a fortress disguised as a home.

Finally, he shows me a cottage-like building right out in the bush. It's stunning, all rustic wood and huge windows, nestled amongst towering gum trees. It looks incredibly quiet, peaceful, and remote. It's a lot like what we just had, but the lack of a visible fence sends a shiver down my spine. The bush is beautiful, but I know now how quickly it can turn into a terrifying, indifferent enemy.

I sigh, leaning my head against his shoulder. "I like the cottage, the quiet of it, but I like the setting of the bigger one. The fence. The proximity to here."

Catcher kisses the top of my head. "We can buy one you like? We can have a fence built around the cottage, or we can buy a big one and customise it. Whatever you want."

I frown, the casualness of his wealth still jarring. "Buy one I like? That's a bit much, Catcher. We don't need to buy a new house."

He kisses my head again, a soft, reassuring pressure.

"Nothing is too much, Posey. Not for you. Not when it comes to your safety."

I settle back into his chest, the weight of the decision too heavy for my tired mind. "You choose. I can't. I just want to be with you."

He puts his phone down, wraps his arms around me, and pulls me in tight. "Get some rest, little bird. I'll handle the choosing. I'll handle everything."

The exhaustion, coupled with the profound safety of his arms, is overwhelming. My eyes slowly droop, and I sleep. The last thing I feel is the steady, strong beat of his heart against my ear, a promise of protection that I finally and completely, believe.

Chapter 29

Catcher

I slip out of the room, leaving Posey curled up in the massive bed. Her hair is spread out around her like a dark, tangled halo, not the good kind. She went to bed with it wet, and now it's a chaotic mess. It's like 11 AM, but the exhaustion from the night before still clings to me like a shroud. I need coffee, and I need a plan that will ensure this never happens again.

I find Aurelio and Gabe in the kitchen. Aurelio is still in his crumpled clothes from last night, the dark fabric clinging to his lean frame. Gabe, however, is in a fresh pair of sweatpants, looking far too composed for the chaos we've just endured. They're cooking breakfast, the smell of frying bacon and eggs is a welcome, domesticated contrast to the violence of the previous hours, and it makes my stomach gurgle in response.

I walk in and sit down heavily at the kitchen island, the cool marble a shock against my skin.

Aurelio looks up from flipping a pancake, his eyes sharp despite the lack of sleep. "I've got an idea."

I run a hand through my short hair, trying to shake the sleep and the lingering fear. "I'm all ears."

"We ask him to fight."

I frown, still half-asleep, the words not registering. "Ask who? What?"

Aurelio rolls his eyes with exaggerated patience. Gabe slides a mug of freshly poured coffee across the counter to me, the ceramic warm in my hand.

"A fight, Catcher," Gabe clarifies, leaning against the counter, his voice low and steady. "We ask Dragon to fight you in the ring tomorrow. In fact, we send the request to Leon."

Gabe's eyes gleam with a predatory intelligence that matches the cold fury in my own gut. "I wouldn't mind getting him in the club, and disposing of him all together. Might as well take the head down so we can make sure we really do run it all."

I take a long, slow sip of the hot coffee, letting the caffeine hit my system. I run a hand down my face, the rough stubble a reminder of the time I've lost. The plan is brutal, efficient, and perfectly tailored to my rage. "Line it up," I say, the words a low growl. "But this is a bit much before I've even taken a fucking piss."

I push myself up from the stool and walk down the hall toward the loo.

Aurelio calls after me as I walk, a smirk audible in his voice. "Well, hurry up! I want to go home to wank and shower, mate!"

I can't help but laugh, a short, sharp bark of amusement. I walk into the loo, and piss, my hand resting on the wall as I aim one-handed. The idea runs through my mind properly now. It's a good idea. A perfect idea. Aurelio and Gabe can deal with Leon while I dispose of his right-hand man. I can get my revenge for him touching my woman, and I can do it in the place where I feel most in control. Dragon Petrovic is mine. And tomorrow, he dies.

I finish and flush the loo, the sound a sharp, final note in the quiet house. I head back to the kitchen, picking my coffee back up and taking a long, grateful gulp. The caffeine is starting to work its magic, sharpening the edges of my mind.

I sit down, the energy returning, and look at my two friends. "Okay, set it up. But maybe we should call Matteo? Or Felix? I mean, if we are going to deal with Leon, we can't dispose of him the same way we do with the fights."

Gabe nods, already pulling out his phone. "I was thinking Felix. We might keep Leon alive for a bit so we can get some information. Felix is good at that."

Aurelio grins, leaning forward, his eyes alight with anticipation. "I'll go with him."

Gabe sighs, a long-suffering sound. "Of course you will." He looks at me, and I just smile, a genuine, appreciative smile.

Gabe taps away at the screen of his phone, putting the call on loudspeaker. It rings twice, a gruff voice answering on the third.

"Gabriel?"

"Morning, Matteo."

"Morning back," Matteo replies, then his voice changes, becoming sharp and parental. "Oi, Niko! You're meant to be doing schoolwork!"

We hear Niko's voice in the background, clear and confident. "I finished it all an hour ago, old man."

"Don't call me old man!" Matteo barks back.

Then a woman's voice cuts in, sweet but firm, Eleanor. "But you are old, darling."

Matteo's voice drops to a low, theatrical growl. "You were not saying that last night when I shoved my dick down your throat."

We all wait, a picture of the domestic chaos painted in our heads, the background banter a strange, comforting rhythm that only our world understands.

Finally, Matteo clears his throat. "Okay, what can I do for you, Gabe?"

Gabe gets straight to the point. "I was wondering if I can borrow Felix tomorrow?"

Matteo goes silent. The silence stretches, thick with thought. "Can I come too?"

Eleanor's voice is immediate and sharp. "No, you can't go too! We have a date booked."

Matteo growls, the sound deep in his chest. "But they want Felix! That means they are doing fun stuff!"

"So taking me out for date night isn't fun?" Eleanor challenges.

Matteo backtracks really fast, his voice suddenly dripping with honey. "No, no, no! That's not what I said at all! I love date night, princess. In fact, I can't wait."

He lowers his voice, speaking quickly to Gabe. "Can you wait a night? I wanna come."

Gabe laughs, a genuine, booming sound. "So you're gonna send Felix then?"

Matteo sighs; a sound of deep, profound disappointment. "Sure. I'll call him now and tell him to head down today. What is going on?"

Gabe tells him about the break-in, and how they are going to set it up as a fight, and then hopefully Leon comes so they can dispose of that issue at the same time.

Matteo's voice is very quiet now, a whisper of regret. "Fuck. I am missing out on fun. God dammit." Then, loudly, he says, "Oh well, I have date night. I'll call Felix for you."

He hangs up. The three of us look at each other, a shared moment of dark amusement.

The plan is set. The pieces moving into place.

It's then Alba walks into the room, rubbing her eyes, wearing a silk dressing gown and fluffy slippers. She walks right past us all, a gracefully silent figure, and heads straight for the coffee machine. Gabe leans against the counter and watches her every move, his expression a mixture of adoration and fierce posses-siveness.

It's only when she stops right in front of him, her head tipping back to look at him, coffee in hand, that he uncrosses his arms and wraps them around her, leaning down to kiss her deeply. The kiss is long and slow, and completely oblivious to the two men watching.

She settles her head on his chest and eyes both Aurelio and me, a small, knowing smile playing on her lips. "Morning, boys."

She lets go of Gabe and walks back out of the room with her coffee in hand, yawning again, the silk robe whis-pering around her legs.

Aurelio shakes his head, a genuine look of wonder on

his face. "I still can't believe you found her after all this time."

Gabe watches her go, then rubs his chest where her head had rested. "Neither can I, mate. But I'm fucking so glad I did. I cannot wait for all this to be over, for it all to be in the past."

Aurelio nods. "It seems to be taking forever, but every time I think on it, I realise how far we have come."

Gabe's expression softens further. "Dad is actually on board with it all now, and Mum is stoked. I think seeing Alba's face again after all those years has made her realise how fucked up our business was. Then she went to work on Dad, who crumbles instantly for her."

I nod, a genuine warmth spreading through me. "It's nice when everyone backs you, mate."

Gabe smiles, a flash of the easy confidence he usually wears. "We can all thank Eleanor. She came up with the whole plan, and it worked well so far."

Chapter 30

Posey

The air in the SUV is thick with a tension that has nothing to do with the twenty new bodyguards Gabe's hired. It's the kind of tension that settles deep in your bones, a cold hard certainty that tonight, something final is going to happen.

I had to beg. I had to use every ounce of the vulnerability Catcher claims to love, every quiet plea I could muster. He had said no, his jaw locked tight, his eyes dark with a fear that mirrored my own. But I couldn't rest; thoughts of that man still breathing, still existing, is a poison in my system. I can't sleep properly until I know he is truly gone, a threat permanently neutralised.

"I can't rest until I know he's gone," I whispered, my voice catching. "I need to see it, Catcher. I need to know you're safe."

That last part is the lie that worked. He's never truly safe, but the idea that my presence could somehow ensure his safety is the key that unlocked his possessiveness. He said yes. Gabe, of course, had then said no, citing the security risk, before Catcher's glare and my quiet persistence wore him down. Twenty more men. That was the compromise.

Alba, however, was not so easily placated. She had made herself very vocally pissed off about being left behind. She paced the living room, her red hair a fiery blur, arguing with Gabe until he finally cornered her, his hands framing her face.

"I can't split my attention, Alba," he'd said, his voice raw. "If I'm worried about you, I might miss something happening to Posey. I need to be focused on Catcher, and I can't do that if you're in the club."

She softened then, the fear for either of us overriding her own stubbornness, and she gave in.

Now, I'm sitting in the back of the black SUV, sandwiched between Catcher and a bodyguard. I'm wearing a pair of tight, dark blue ripped jeans that Alba bought me, and an oversized t-shirt. The shirt is black, and across the chest, a massive skeletal style Grim Reaper, with a scythe in hand, surrounded by a swirling vortex of smoke.

The irony isn't lost on me. Not in the slightest. This is the top Catcher grabbed from the pile of clothes I had in my room. He chose the Grim Reaper for me.

I run a hand over the soft cotton, the image of death cool beneath my fingertips. My heart isn't racing with fear anymore. It's beating with a cold, steady rhythm that feels alien and powerful. I am here to watch a man who tried to take me away from my cage, from my safe space, be destroyed. And the terrifying thing is, I want to see it. I need to see it.

I look out the window at the flashing city lights, the

world a blur of motion and colour. I'm no longer the girl who was dragged here. I'm the woman who has been claimed; and tonight, my claim will be sealed in blood. The Grim Reaper on my chest feels less like a warning, Catcher is coming.

The SUV glides to a stop right outside the club's entrance, a spot usually reserved for Catcher's car, but tonight, it's for all of us. Gabe, who is driving, kills the engine. Aurelio, in the front passenger seat, is already scanning the crowd. Catcher, me, and a bodyguard named Joey are in the back.

Catcher gets out first, his movements fluid and coiled, a predator stepping into his domain. His hand immediately finding mine, his touch an anchor.

We walk in, and the heat hits me first, the combined warmth of a thousand bodies, sweat, and adrenaline. The noise is a physical thing, a roaring wave of yelling and cheering that makes the very air vibrate. The place is packed, a sea of faces pressed against the railings, all here for the main event that has been arranged so quickly, it's almost laughable. They accepted the fight so damn quickly, a sign of either arrogance or desperation from Leon. Gabe sent the request, and Leon accepted.

We haven't taken ten steps when a tall man walks up to us. He's massive, easily a six-foot-four wall of muscle that's similar to Catcher's build. He's covered in just as many tattoos as Catcher, with intricate black ink swirling up his neck and disappearing under the collar of his pristine three-piece suit. His black hair is a thick mop, styled so perfectly it looks like it was sculpted. His eyes, however, are what stop me, they gleam with pure unadulterated, death. He has to be one of the bodyguards.

But the second Gabe and Aurelio see him, their hard edges soften. They throw their arms around him, a genuine, bone-crushing hug, followed by a kiss on the cheek.

"Felix!" Gabe booms, his voice full of relief.

"Gabe, Aurelio," Felix replies, his voice a low rumble that barely cuts through the crowd noise.

He turns to Catcher, who does the same quick, but fierce embrace. Catcher then pushes me forward, his hand resting firmly on the small of my back.

"This is Posey."

Felix holds out his hand, his palm rough and calloused. "Hello, Posey. Welcome to the family. I'm Felix." He flashes a grin at me; it's all teeth and sends a shiver up my spine.

I manage a small smile back, but I can feel my own heart rate speed up. This man is dangerous, a different kind of dangerous than Catcher. Catcher is a storm; Felix is the silent, inevitable earthquake. I have no idea why, but I know it to be true.

Catcher claps Felix on the shoulder. "Happy hunting."

Felix nods, his eyes already scanning the crowd.

Catcher steers me toward the changing rooms, the private corridor a sudden, blessed relief from the noise. Aurelio follows, already pulling the wraps from his bag.

"Who is staying with Posey while you hunt?" Catcher asks Aurelio as we stop at a bench seat and get ready, his voice tight with concern.

Aurelio doesn't even look up as he starts wrapping

Catcher's hand. "Michael, Peter, Dean, and Justin will surround her. Then there is another five behind her."

Catcher pushes his lips out, a silent protest.

Aurelio looks up, his eyes meeting Catcher's. "Once Felix leaves, I'll be right back at her side."

Catcher nods, a small concession. I just stand and listen, the conversation a strange, detached reality.

Catcher gets changed quickly, his movements economical and focused as he strips down to a pair of black fighting shorts, the fabric clinging to his powerful thighs. I watch him, unashamedly, as he moves. His body is perfection; a sculpture carved from granite and sinew. Who would have thought a body that ripped and that hard would make someone soften like I did for him? He is a rock, a boulder; yet for me, he's a teddy bear, and I love it. I love him.

Aurelio starts oiling up his chest, the slick sheen of the oil catching the harsh overhead light, highlighting every ridge and valley of his muscles. Catcher grins at me while I continue to watch him, his eyes holding a fierce pride.

Once Catcher is ready, his hand reaches for mine. I kiss both his wrapped knuckles, the cotton rough on my lips. He pulls me close to him, his breath warm against my ear.

"Let's go kill one of our demons, little bird."

There is a frantic, excited energy about him now, a pure unadulterated joy, that is infectious. It's clear this is where Catcher feels the most at home, the happiest, and most settled. I get it. The world goes quiet for me when I train, the noise of my past fades into the rhythm of my breath and my movements. So, for him in this arena, it must be nothing but dust bunnies.

We leave the changing rooms and settle into the ring-side seats, the guards immediately forming a silent, impenetrable wall around us. Aurelio bumps knuckles with him and takes off, leaving me and Catcher with all the guards standing there, waiting for his turn.

Catcher leans down into my face and kisses me deeply, a kiss that is both a promise and a goodbye. He pulls back just enough for his lips to brush my ear, his voice a low growl over the noise of the club.

"I love you, Posey. You will be Mrs. Calcone after this."

I just nod at him, my heart swelling with a fierce, terrifying joy. "Yes," I say, my voice steady. "I will be."

He smiles at me, a genuine, blinding smile that makes the chaos around us disappear.

Gabe returns to us, his face serious. "You're up in five, Catcher."

Chapter 31

Catcher

The roar of the crowd is a wave of sound and heat that slams into me as I step through the ropes. It's a symphony of bloodlust and anticipation, but tonight, it's just noise. I'm already in the zone, a cold, empty space where only the target exists. The canvas is cool and slightly sticky under my bare feet.

My gaze snaps past the blinding lights, past the faces blurred by adrenaline and cheap booze, straight to her. Posey. She's caged within a sea of guards, but she's the only thing I see. My anchor. My reason. I won't look away. Not until that fuckwit is locked in here with me. She's wearing that ridiculous Grim Reaper shirt that Alba bought her, I've seen her wear it a few times since she got it, it was why I grabbed it to start with it.

Her hand lifts, a small and delicate movement, and she blows me a kiss. It's a silent prayer, a tiny spark of light in this dark pit. The hard, cold shell around my heart cracks, just for a second. A breath of warmth. God, I love this woman. She's all fire and fear, a contradiction that makes her the strongest thing I've ever known. She's strong and capable of a lot, a survivor who's faced down a monster and didn't break. But she's also soft and needs me, and I need to be needed. I need to be her shield, her fortress. I'm going to burn this world down and rebuild it for her. She will not know anything but love every day once this is over. The thought is a vow; a promise forged in the heat of this moment.

A body starts to climb through the ropes snagging my attention away from my future and back to the filth of the present. Dragon Petrovic saunters up, like the grotesque parody of a man he is. He catches my eye and grins; his slash of a mouth extending wide and confidently, making my blood run cold with pure, unadulterated hatred. He thinks this is a game. He actually thinks he has a chance.

The announcer's voice booms over the speakers, a distorted god-like sound reverberating through the warehouse, "Ladies and gentlemen! Are you ready for the main event of the evening?" The crowd screams, a guttural, hungry sound. "Tonight, we have a score to settle! In the blue corner, our undefeated champion, the King of Melbourne, Catcher Calcone!" I raise a fist, a practiced, empty gesture for the crowd. My eyes never leave Dragon. "And in the red corner, making his debut, the challenger, Dragon Petrovic!"

"Has everyone placed their bets?" the announcer continues, his voice dripping with showmanship. "Catcher is our undefeated champion here."

I tune out the rest. The words blurring into a meaningless drone. All that matters is the man across from me. My eyes land on Dragon's and hold his stare. The hate running through me is strong, a coil of muscle tightening in my gut. He touched what is mine. He hurt her. He will pay for every bruise, every tear, every moment of fear he inflicted. This piece of shit is dead.

We move to the centre. The referee, a thick-set man with a face like granite, gives us the final instructions. I don't hear them. I just nod, my focus a laser beam on Dragon.

The announcer's voice cuts through the final time. "Is everyone ready... good. Over to you, Ref."

The man stands between us like a temporary barrier as he raises his hand, waiting for the final moment of silence, and then blows his whistle.

The sound is sharp and final. The referee steps back.

We start to circle. My eyes are locked on his, calculating and cold. We both know this isn't a match; it's an execution. Dragon lunges first, a wild, desperate energy to his movements. He's sloppy, fuelled by rage and a misplaced sense of entitlement. I dodge, the wind of his heavy fist whipping past my ear, and counter with a sharp jab to his ribs. He grunts, but the hit doesn't slow him. He's bigger than his dead twin; a slab of muscle and hate.

He presses the attack, a flurry of untrained but powerful swings. I'm faster and cleaner; my movements honed by years of discipline, but he's relentless. He catches me with a glancing blow to the temple. The lights in the arena flicker, and a hot, metallic taste floods my mouth. He has the upper hand for a bit. I stumble back, shaking my head to clear the suddenly blinding fog. The crowd noise swells; a hungry beast smelling blood.

Then, I hear it. A sound that cuts through the roar, a sound that rips me out of the haze.

"CATCHER! SHAKE IT OFF! GET HIM!"

It's Posey. Her voice, raw and terrified, is a whip-crack across my consciousness. It's not a plea for me to win; it's a command to survive. It's the sound of my future, my everything, demanding I don't fail.

The fog vanishes. The pain is a distant hum. My focus snaps back, sharper than before. He made her scream. He made her afraid. That is his final mistake.

I meet his next charge head-on. He throws a right hook; I duck under it, my shoulder slamming into his gut, driving the air from his lungs. He doubles over, and I seize the moment. My elbow comes down in a brutal, bone-jarring strike to the back of his neck. The force of the blow is immense, a focused explosion of all the rage, all the love, all the promises I've made.

Dragon drops. He hits the mat with a sickening thud, his body instantly slack. He's not out, not yet, but he's broken. He tries to push himself up, his eyes wide and unfocused, a look of pure, animalistic panic finally replacing the arrogant grin.

I don't give him a chance. I straddle his chest, pinning him to the canvas. The crowd is a distant, hysterical shriek. All I see is the face of the man who put his hands on my woman.

My fist comes down. Once. Twice. The sound is sickeningly wet. I hear the crunch of bone, the tearing of flesh.

I'm the monster I need to be right now, the one who loves the sound of death in my ears.

I keep hitting him. I don't stop. I can feel the soft give of his skull, the way his face collapses under the relentless, piston-like force of my blows. I'm past rage. I'm in a cold, necessary void. This isn't about winning a fight. This is about erasing a threat. This is about justice for the fear he put in her eyes.

My knuckles are screaming, but I love the pain, it's grounding. I feel the wet, pulpy resistance, the final, shuddering stop of his body beneath me. I hit him until there is nothing left. Smashing his face in with my fist till there is nothing at all left of him.

I pull my hand back, finally. I look down. The mat is slick, dark red, and something else. White and grey. Brain matter on the mat and his hands.

I rise slowly, my chest heaving, the blood dripping from my hands, painting the canvas. The silence is deafening, a suddenly heavy blanket over the thousands of people. Then it's loud, as everyone starts cheering at the death they now see; the very thing they came to see.

My eyes find Posey. She's standing, her hands clamped over her mouth, her eyes wide, but she's not looking away. She's looking at me. I had hoped she would close her eyes again, but I think she needed to see this man die to find peace; so, I don't get upset, instead I puff out my chest knowing that I've given her peace, in the only way I know how.

I walk to the edge of the ring, bloodied and breathing hard. I reach through the ropes, my hand, still dripping, I reach for her.

She doesn't flinch. She doesn't hesitate. She takes my hand, her small, warm fingers closing around my sore, bloody ones.

"It's over, mia cara," I rasp, my voice raw. "It's done."

Then I watch in pure horror as her eyes roll into the back of her head and she collapses, one of the bodyguards instantly reaching out to catch her.

Chapter 32

Gabriel

The cheering is a constant, deafening wave, a perfect cover for what Aurelio and I are doing. We slink through the club, moving against the current of the frenzied crowd, our bodies pressed close to the shadows of the concrete walls. Every step is measured, every breath shallow. This is the real fight; one Catcher can't win with his fists.

I can hear the cheering, the collective gasp and roar that tells me Catcher is either dominating or taking a hit. I don't need to see it. My focus is on the back corner, the quiet eye of this storm.

And there they are. Leon Alexander and his third, positioned perfectly. They're leaning against a cement pillar, their attention fixed on the cage, oblivious to the two shadows closing in.

Leon is exactly as I pictured him: a man who has grown soft on the spoils of his violence. He's a big man, not muscle-bound like Catcher, but thick, with a heavy, expensive suit that strains across his shoulders. The suit is a dark, charcoal grey, a poor attempt to blend into the shadows, but the silk tie and the gold watch flashing under the arena lights betray his arrogance. His hair is slicked back, silver at the temples, and his face is a mask of cold, calculating expectation. He looks like a CEO of a legitimate business; which is exactly what makes him so dangerous. He's here to watch his dog fight, to enjoy the spectacle of his revenge. He's too confident.

His man, the third in charge, is a different beast. He's younger, maybe early thirties, lean and wired tight. He's wearing a simple black t-shirt and jeans; his arms a roadmap of amateur tattoos, already fading. His head is shaved, and his eyes, even from this distance, are flat and dead. He's a soldier, a tool, and he's positioned himself slightly behind Leon, a human shield waiting for a command. He's the one I'm worried about, the one who might have a twitchy finger.

I check the perimeter. All our guards are surrounding this place tonight. They're scattered through the crowd, indistinguishable from the other lowlifes, but their eyes are on us. Even if Leon brought some, mine will step in before they can do anything. The knowledge is a cold comfort. We have the numbers, the element of surprise, and the absolute necessity of success.

I catch Aurelio's eye. He's a ghost in the dark, his movements fluid and silent. He's already holding a knife in his hand, the blade catching in the distant light; a silent promise of death. It's a thin, wicked thing, designed for silence and speed.

I give him a small, almost imperceptible nod. The signal.

He responds by holding up three fingers and stares me down. Three seconds. That's all the time we have. Three seconds to cover the distance, three seconds to silence them both, three seconds before the chaos of the crowd turns on us.

We drop lower, creeping up behind the men. The roar from the crowd peaks, a collective scream of shock or triumph. It's the perfect distraction.

My heart isn't pounding. It's a steady, cold drumbeat in my chest. I taste the dust and the adrenaline. I can smell Leon's expensive cologne, a sickly-sweet scent of power and decay.

Three.

Aurelio is a whisper of motion to my left. His target is the soldier.

Two.

I pull the wire from my sleeve, the thin metal cold and unforgiving against my palm. Leon's thick neck is waiting.

One.

The crowd explodes again. It's time.

We rush the men. It's a silent, practiced blur of motion. Aurelio is a phantom, covering the ground between him and the man in a single, terrifying stride. The man barely has time to register the movement before Aurelio is on him.

I see the flash of steel, and then Aurelio's face. He smiles, a wide, feral and utterly disturbing grin that stretches his features. His knife is drawn across the man's neck in a swift, clean arc. A dark, thick line appearing, and then the blood; it doesn't just drip, it arches out and down his chest, a crimson fountain against the black t-shirt. The soldier doesn't speak, the only sound, a gurgling, wet noise as his life drains out. Aurelio catches the spray on his hand, and the smile on the man's face as his hand is covered in the blood, is disturbing. He looks like a child who just got away with the ultimate prank.

I wait one more second as Leon, alerted by the sudden silence next to him, turns to his third. His mouth opens to shout; a question, a warning, a curse, it doesn't matter. The second is all I need.

I swing the wire up and over the top of his head, wrapping it around his throat and pull, hard. The thin wire bites deep into the soft flesh of his neck, cutting off his air and his scream. His eyes bulge; the calculating look replaced by pure, desperate terror. His hands instantly start to claw at his neck, clawing uselessly at the wire as his expensive suit jacket bunches up around his shoulders.

Just as his knees begin to buckle, a shadow detaches itself from the deeper darkness and Felix saunters out of the shadows. He's wearing a ridiculous three-piece suit, looking completely unbothered by the carnage. He doesn't say a word, moving with a cold, efficient grace. He helps me to zip tie Leon's hands behind his back, and also his ankles.

I keep the pressure on the wire, the fight leaving Leon's body, until he's a limp, choked out, sack of meat. Then, letting go of the wire, I wrap it back up and tuck it into my pocket. I didn't kill him. I want to keep him alive. I have a few questions to ask the fuckwit before Felix goes to town on him.

He grabs the man's upper body and I take the legs; we carry him out to the waiting van Felix brought. We don't bother with subtlety now. The crowd is still focused on the ring, and our men are running interference. We throw him in the back with a heavy, satisfying thud.

Aurelio is right behind us, dragging the dead third by an ankle. The body leaving a dark, wet trail on the concrete. We throw his dead body in too, right next to Leon who is already struggling against the zip ties. I slam the door shut.

Felix holds out a clean, white rag for Aurelio who just smiles and says no thanks. He looks down at his blood-soaked hand, then back at Felix. Felix raises a brow but doesn't say a word.

A sudden, sharp silence falls over the club. The cheering stops. It's the kind of silence that means something definitive has happened in the ring.

"You better get back in there," Felix says, his voice low and even. "Sounds like the fight is done."

I turn on my heels and rush in. There is no way Catcher didn't win, but the adrenaline in my body is pumping and the fear is creeping in.

I rush to the ring, shoving past bodies, my eyes scanning the scene. I see Catcher standing, bloodied but whole, and the relief is instant. He's at the edge of the ring, reaching out, waiting for Posey to grab his hand; which she does without any hesitation.

Then, I watch as she collapses.

Catcher doesn't hesitate. He shoves himself through the ropes at her, becoming a frantic, bloody blur. The crowd is a mess of noise again, but all I can hear is the frantic pounding of my own heart. What the fuck happened.

Chapter 33

Catcher

The world goes silent. One second, she's there, her small, warm hand in my bloody one, her eyes wide with relief. The next, she's gone. Her knees buckle, and she crumples like a puppet with its strings cut.

"Posey!"

The roar of the crowd, the body being dragged away behind me, it all fades to a dull, distant thrum. My focus is absolute, my vision becoming a tunnel of pure, unadulterated terror. I slip through the ropes like a blood covered blur.

I scoop Posey out of the arms of the guard who caught her, my arms sliding under her, lifting her slight weight against my chest. She's limp, a dead weight, and the sight of her pale, still face is a punch to the gut; worse than anything Dragon threw at me. I check her pulse against her neck, a frantic, desperate press of my thumb. Thump-thump. Thump-thump. It's there, weak but steady. She's just passed out.

I don't stop to explain, don't stop to look back. I grab the gun, I stashed, off the guard and tuck it into the waistband of my shorts. Then, I run to the change rooms with her. I move through the chaos of the back halls like a man possessed, her body a precious, fragile burden. Every step a prayer, a curse, a promise; if she's okay, I'll never let her out of my sight again.

Bursting into the tiled, sterile room, I lay her down on the bench seat; the same bench where I prepared for the fight and where I told her she'd be Mrs. Calcone. The irony is a bitter taste in my mouth.

I drop to my knees beside her, my bloody hands running all over her trying to work out what happened. I check her head for a bump, her limbs for a break. I peel back her eyelids, her pupils are dilated, but equal. What the fuck is wrong?

"Posey? Little Bird? Wake up," I rasp, my voice unrecognisable. I cup her face, my thumb brushing her cheek. The blood from my hands smearing across her perfect skin; like a grotesque, crimson war paint.

The door slams open.

I react on instinct. My hand rushes to my waist, pulling the gun free. I spin; the cold steel levelled at the two figures framed in the doorway.

"Get the fuck out!" I snarl, my finger tightening on the trigger.

They freeze. Gabe and Aurelio. They both hold their hands up instantly, recognising the wild, cornered animal in my eyes.

I stare at them for a long, agonising second, the gun trembling slightly as the red haze from the fight still clouds my vision, and for a moment, they're just more threats. Then, the fog clears. It's Gabe. It's Aurelio. My brothers.

I lower the gun, the barrel pointing at the floor, the metallic click of the safety a loud punctuation mark in the sudden silence.

Gabe rushes forward, his eyes darting from me to Posey. "What the fuck happened?" he demands, his voice tight with alarm.

I shake my head, my focus already back on her. "I'm not sure," I say, my voice flat, devoid of the rage that just minutes ago was a living thing. I place the gun back in my waistband and go back to checking her over, my hands moving with a desperate but gentle urgency. I lift her wrist, feeling for the pulse again, counting the beats. "She just collapsed. Shock, maybe. She saw everything."

Aurelio moves to the door, his eyes scanning the hall. Gabe kneels on the other side of the bench, his hand resting on her ankle.

Gabe's voice is low, urgent. "What do you want to do?"

I don't look up, my focus still on her pale face. "I'm not sure," I admit, the words a raw whisper. My mind is a blank slate, the tactical genius of the fight gone, replaced by a primal, animal fear. I can handle a knife fight, a gun battle, a cage match.

I can't handle this.

It's then I see it. A dark, wet spot on the old tile floor, directly beneath the bench. It's growing, slowly, steadily. My eyes track the source. The blood is seeping through the ripped denim of her jeans, through the thin gap in the bench slats, and starts to drip onto the floor through the bench seat. It's not the dark, clotted blood from my knuck-les. This is bright, fresh, terrifyingly red.

My breath hitches. My hands fly back to her hips, checking for a wound, a tear, anything. There's nothing on the outside, but the blood is definitely coming from her.

"Gabe," I say, my voice a low, dangerous growl. "Gabe, look."

He follows my gaze to the floor, and his eyes widen. The silent question hangs heavy in the air.

I don't wait for an answer. My panic is a cold, sharp spike in my chest. I scoop her up again, cradling her against my blood-soaked body. The fight is over, but the war for her is just beginning.

"Forget the plan," I bark, my voice echoing off the tiles. "We're going to the hospital now!"

I push past Gabe, my focus fixed on the door, on the outside, on getting her help. Aurelio barks orders on his phone as we race for the SUV and pile in. I jump into the back seat with Posey in my arms, cradling her head against my chest, trying to shield her from the rough handling. Gabe takes the wheel.

Aurelio is a machine. I hear him tell Felix to have fun, that they have an emergency, and then he hangs up. He immediately calls our resident doctor and tells him to get to emergency now. "Anthony, you have five minutes. I don't care where you are. You fucking better get there before we do, we pay you enough to do it."

The SUV lurches as Gabe backs out of the parking space and races to the hospital, driving like a mad man. The world outside is a blur of Melbourne street-lights and speed. I'm slammed against the door, but I don't care. I think he needs to go faster. I press my lips to Posey's forehead, whispering useless reassurances.

The second Gabe slams the brakes on in the emergency bay, I'm moving. I don't wait for the sliding doors to open. I kick them open and I'm running inside, Posey in my arms, barking at the nurses for help.

I must look like a monster. I'm only in fighting shorts, my body a canvas of sweat and blood. My hands and chest are covered in bloody splatter and brain matter; a grotesque trophy from the cage. But again, I don't give a shit. All that matters is the dead weight in my arms.

The nurses at the desk race out to help, their eyes wide with shock and alarm. One, a woman with sharp, intelligent eyes and a no-nonsense bun, is the first to reach me. She's already pulling on gloves.

"Sir, what happened?" she asks, her voice surprisingly calm.

"I have no idea, she collapsed," I growl, my voice raw. "Doctor Anthony Murry is on his way."

The nurse frowns at me but doesn't argue the name. "Okay, we need to get her into a bed now."

I clutch Posey tighter, my arms locked around her. I can't let her go. Not yet. Not to strangers.

"Sir, you will need to put her down," the nurse says, her tone hardening. "I need to check her vitals."

I growl, a low, guttural sound, I pull her closer, my chin resting on her head. *Mine.*

The nurse doesn't flinch. She stands her ground, her eyes meeting mine, utterly unafraid. She leads me to a nearby trauma bed. "Put her down here now, sir. I need to check her over. Do not be the reason she doesn't make it cause you're being an over possessive Alpha-hole."

Alpha-hole. The shock of her audacity and the sheer, cold truth of her accusation is enough to break through my panic. She's right. I'm wasting time.

I place her down gently on the crisp white sheets.

The nurse immediately gets to work, her fingers flying to Posey's wrist and neck. Her eyes, however, are fixed on the growing stain on the sheets. She sees the blood.

"When did the bleeding start?" she asks, her voice sharp.

"A little after she passed out," I say, my voice trembling slightly. "I have no idea where it's coming from."

The nurse looks at me, a grim certainty in her eyes. She doesn't say a word. She just grabs a pair of trauma shears and starts to cut her jeans off her with a decisive snip.

As the denim parts, she looks up at me, her expression unreadable. "I have an idea."

Chapter 34

Posey

The first thing I register is the smell: sterile antiseptic; a cold, clean scent that is the antithesis of the fight club's grime. The second is the dull, heavy ache in my lower abdomen; a hollow, empty feeling that has nothing to do with pain. I blink, my eyelids feeling impossibly heavy, as the white ceiling of the hospital room swims into focus.

My hand is warm. Impossibly warm. I turn my head slowly on the pillow, and my breath catches.

Catcher.

He's sitting beside the bed, leaning forward, his large hand completely engulfing mine. He's not wearing the blood-soaked shorts from the cage. His hair is still damp, slicked back from his forehead, and he's wearing plain scrubs, a pale blue that does nothing to hide the sheer, raw power of him. The fabric strains at his shoulders, the cotton stretched taut over the mountains of muscle I know so intimately. He looks out of place, a dangerous feral thing caged in a sterile box, and yet, he's here. He's whole. He's safe.

And he's fussing over me like crazy. His eyes, usually so hard and cold, are soft, darting over my face, checking every tiny twitch. He looks exhausted, the shadows under his eyes dark and bruised.

It's surprisingly hot as fuck. The sight of him, cleaned up but still radiating that potent energy, makes a slow, deep warmth spread through my chest.

I lift my free hand, my fingers trembling slightly, and touch his face. The stubble is a rough grounding texture under my palm. He leans into the touch, closing his eyes for a brief, silent moment of relief.

He opens his eyes and smiles, a small, tender curve of his lips that is only ever for me. "Do you need anything, little bird?" he rasps, his voice low and thick with emotion.

I manage a small smile back. The words are a struggle, but they're true. "No, I'm fine."

I had woken up not long after we arrived, confused, and naked from the waist down; there was blood everywhere, and Catcher was a complete mess.

The door opens, and the moment shatters. And the memory of waking up fades along with it.

A man walks in, a crisp, professional figure in a white coat. This is Doctor Anthony Murry; he'd arrived a few minutes after we had and taken over my care. He looks tired; but composed.

Catcher stands instantly, his entire posture shifting from tender lover to demanding king. He steps slightly in front of me, a protective wall.

"What's the verdict," Catcher says, his voice devoid of any softness, all business.

The doctor doesn't flinch at Catcher's intensity. He walks to the foot of the bed, his hands clasped professionally.

"Well, as you know, you have had a miscarriage, Mrs. Calcone," he says, his tone clinical and direct. The title, Mrs. Calcone, hangs in the air; a cruel echo of Catcher's proposal just hours ago. The word miscarriage bounces around in my mind like a ping pong ball; in fact, it's been popping around in there since he told me hours ago.

"The ultrasound has all come back clear," Dr. Murry continues, flipping through a chart. "We don't need to do a D&C. Your body has handled the loss naturally. You're physically stable. You can go home today if you want." My eyes fill up with tears as I look at him. The grief is a quiet, heavy weight, not a sudden explosion. I didn't know I was pregnant, but the knowledge of the loss is still a deep, aching wound. I manage a shaky whisper. "Thank you, Doctor."

Catcher, ever the pragmatist, cuts straight to the heart of his fear, the one thing I didn't want to think about. He asks the one thing I didn't want to, his voice rough, "So, she is okay down there, right? She can still fall pregnant again if she wants to?"

The doctor smiles at him, a genuinely kind expression that softens his clinical demeanour. "Yes, the ultrasound showed nothing abnormal at all. The easiest explanation is that your body cleaned house. It's why you bled so much, so quickly. I know it can seem like a lot of blood, but I promise you, it wasn't as much as one would think, it's just spreads so suddenly and looks scary. Your body will need a few weeks of healing."

Catcher nods, absorbing the technical details, but his eyes are still clouded with a deeper question. He asks, his voice barely a whisper, "Then why did it happen?"

Dr. Murry sighs, his gaze turning serious. "Miscarriages can happen for many reasons. Some can be because the body simply wasn't ready, or there was something wrong with the baby itself. We never really know at this stage, but my guess is that the shot you have been taking is still working its way out of your body, making you unable to carry a child yet. If you are to take the shot again, I would recommend taking it on time and not missing it, or to not try for a baby for another few months so your body has the chance to make sure the drug is out of your system completely."

I nod at him, because that makes perfectly terrifying sense. I was due for the next shot, and I hadn't taken it. It was the reason.

The doctor gives us a final, gentle smile. "I'll leave you two. A nurse will be in shortly with your discharge papers."

It's only when he leaves that Catcher's shoulders slump. The protective wall he built around himself crumbles, and he looks utterly defeated. He sinks back into the chair; his eyes fixed on the white sheet.

"I shouldn't have taken you to the club," he says, his voice thick with self-blame. "All that stress and worry... it was too much."

I reach out, my hand finding the front of his scrub top and pull him towards me. He comes willingly, collapsing against my side, his head resting on my shoulder. I run my fingers through his damp hair, the gesture a silent balm.

"It's not your fault, baby, or mine," I whisper, my own tears finally falling, running paths down my face. "It's just life."

He pulls back just enough to look at me, his eyes red-rimmed and vulnerable. The mean, forthright king is gone, replaced by a man who is utterly lost.

"I was so not ready for a child," he confesses, the words tearing from his throat. "But now that I had one... I want one."

"I know I feel the same, baby." I voice my own truth.

He rests his head back down, burrowing into my neck; his breath warm against my skin. The admission hangs in the air, a new, fragile promise between us.

"Let's go the fuck home," he says, his voice muffled and thick with exhaustion. "I'm so tired."

I kiss his damp hair, the scent of hospital soap and Catcher a comforting mix. "Ok, baby."

Chapter 35

Posey

2 Years Later

The sun is a warm, heavy blanket on my skin, as I settle deeper into the crazy ass chair Catcher got me for sitting out in the sun; it's a ridiculously oversized rattan swing chair with cushions that feel like clouds. I close my eyes, letting the heat soak into my bones. It's been two years since Catcher took me from the warehouse, two years since the blood, the fear and the loss. Two years of quiet, steady healing.

I sit for 30 minutes, just relaxing as the morning sun warms my body. It's my ritual, my moment of peace before the day begins. The silence here is profound, broken only by the distant call of a kookaburra, a sound that now makes me smile.

Catcher found the perfect house. It's this massive thing

just up the road from Alba and Gabe's, a sprawling, modern fortress of glass and stone, but it has a lot more land around it than the other one. Acres of thick, native bushland giving us a sense of complete isolation. Catcher had it fully fenced in; a high, impenetrable perimeter that whispers of his constant need for security. He told me to do anything I wanted with the inside, and so I have.

I've spent the last two years schmoozing and creating magical spaces inside, room by room. It feels freeing being able to create my own sanctuary over and over again. Each room is a reflection of a different part of me; a bold and dark study, an airy light-filled kitchen, and a bedroom that is pure, unadulterated luxury. Catcher never hates anything I do, in fact, he is always in awe with each room as I reveal them. He walks in, his eyes wide, and just says, "Perfect, little bird. Absolutely perfect." His approval is the only one that matters.

Life has settled into a rhythm. Alba has become one of my closest friends. We go to each other's house a lot, trading stories and sharing coffee in the massive, sun-drenched outdoor areas. The men work all the time, consumed by the endless dark business of their world, so it is nice to have someone to talk to during the day. Alba understands the strange, gilded cages we live in, the constant presence of security, and the unspoken rules.

And Catcher? He's still an over-protective alpha-hole who follows my every movement, but I don't seem to mind. His possessiveness is a language of love I've come to understand. He's the shadow at my back, the silent guard at the door. He's the one who makes sure the sun is warm and the chair is comfortable. He's the one who gives me peace.

I open my eyes, stretching languidly in the sun. I am safe. I am loved. I am home.

I hear footsteps heading towards me, slow and deliberate, the sound of expensive leather on polished stone. I don't need to look up to know who it is. Catcher rounds the chair and stands in front of me, blocking the sun. His shadow is a welcome, familiar weight.

I move over for him to sit, shifting my weight to the side of the swing chair. He settles in behind me, his massive body a perfect, warm curve against my back. He hands me a cup of tea, the porcelain warm against my fingers. His body curls around mine, and his hand, scarred and powerful, lands on the growing belly I now sport.

After the miscarriage, we didn't try to stop from falling pregnant. We didn't try at all, really. It was a silent, mutual agreement that it just didn't happen, and I had told Catcher that it would happen when the time was right. And it has.

The time was right a few weeks after Catcher came home from work and declared they had done it. They had achieved their goal. No more trafficking in Victoria. Gabe is only one man, he can't control the rest of Australia, but he does control Victoria, and they did it. Now the women who arrive are given three choices. Many choose to work for Gabe. Gabe has bought up so much real estate now in Melbourne city, needing to give them all somewhere to work. They are also sent to Sydney and Brisbane for Ricci and Rossi to give jobs to. Some even choose to be sold to men as wives, but they are monitored, checked up on to make sure they are treated well. The need for mail-order brides is massive in Australia, something I never thought was a thing, but hey, here we are. And some are just let go, free to get their own job, sort out their own lives. What they do once they leave is in their own hands.

It was this catalyst that found me pregnant. A few weeks after that win, I found myself throwing up non-stop, and Catcher fussing over me like a mother hen. It was sweet, although his protective nature is now 100x worse. I used to be able to go to Albas during the day with one guard, now I have four. He won't let me out of his sight when he is around, and he has one hand on my belly at all times, like the presence of it will simply be the only shield it needs. I love it. I adore Catcher.

He leans down, his lips brushing my ear. "Little bird, what do you want to do today? I have the day off, and I would love to spend it with you."

I smile at him and turn my head to kiss him deeply. "Oh good, cause I have three jobs for you."

He frowns, pulling back slightly. "What are they?"

"I need a cot put together, and a change table, and a rug dragged into the baby's room."

"Why do you keep buying flat packs, little bird? You know I hate them," he grumbles, the sound rumbling through my back.

"It's not my fault they come that way," I say, trying to suppress a giggle.

"Why can't you buy them pre-built?"

"They never had that option," I say, tracing the line of his jaw. "Plus, I have you!"

He leans in and kisses me deeply again. "Fine." He stands, pulling me up with him. He holds out his hand, his eyes shining with a mixture of exasperation and love. "Let's go build flat packs, Mrs. Calcone."

The End

Bonus Chapter - Catcher

The air in the warehouse is cold and damp, smelling of stale concrete, iron, and fear. It's a palpable thing, this kind of fear is a high-pitched whine beneath the silence, far removed from the sweaty, chaotic bloodlust of the fight club. This is where the real work happens; the necessary evil that keeps the rest of our world turning.

I stand in the doorway, letting my eyes adjust to the dim, single-bulb light hanging precariously from a ceiling beam, that's 20 feet above us . The light is weak, casting long, dancing shadows that make the empty space feel vast and menacing, like the belly of some great big, sleeping beast. The concrete floor is cracked and stained, the cold seeping right through the soles of my boots.

My mind is a strange, quiet place. Just yesterday, I was a savage, my hands buried in the soft tissue of a man's skull. Now, I'm here, to watch Felix be executioner to the man who sent that savage to my door. The contrast isn't lost on me, but the motivation is the same: Posey. Every act of violence, every calculated cruelty, is a brick in the wall I build around her. I think of her pale face on the hospital bed, the terrifying blood and the word miscarriage. The cold rage that fuelled the fight was still a low, steady burn; but now it's focused, honed to a razor's edge. This isn't about revenge anymore; it's about eradication. It's about ensuring that nothing like this ever touches her again.

In the centre of the room, Leon Alexander is strung up. He's hanging from a thick chain, his hands zip-tied tightly above his head, his feet barely skimming the floor. The chain groans softly with his weight. He's stripped down to just his expensive trousers, the suit shirt and jacket from the club long gone, revealing a soft, pasty torso that hasn't seen a day of honest work or sun. The skin is pale, almost translucent, a perfect canvas for what is to come. He's breathing is hard, the panic from the van ride and the sudden, jarring suspension for the past day, taking its toll. His eyes are wide, darting around the room, searching for an escape that doesn't exist.

Felix is there. He's changed out of his three-piece suit and into something more practical: black tactical gear that somehow still looks tailored. He's polishing a wicked-looking hunting knife with a piece of silk, the blade catching the weak light with a mesmerisingly, deadly flash. He looks like a bored artist waiting for his model to pose.

Gabe and Aurelio walk in behind me, their footsteps echoing on the concrete floor. Gabe flashes me a sad smile, and Aurelio is humming a tune a I can't place.

"Well, well," I say, my voice echoing in the vast space.

I walk slowly toward Leon, my boots crunching on something small and metallic, a discarded zip tie. I kick it aside. "Look what the cat dragged in. The great Leon Alexander. You look… uncomfortable. Did you enjoy the show?"

Leon lifts his head, his eyes bloodshot and wide with a desperate hope that I might be merciful. "You won't get away with this. My people,"

I backhand him across the face. Hard. The sound a sharp, wet crack that silences his protest, the force snaps his head back against the chain.

"Your people are either dead, or running for their lives," I correct him, my voice low and dangerous, each word a hammer blow. "And you are in our house, on my time. You will speak when spoken to, and you will answer every question. Understand?"

Leon spits a mouthful of blood and a broken tooth onto the floor. "Go to hell."

I look at Felix, a slow, deliberate turn of my head. "He's got spirit. I like that. Don't take it all at once, Felix. We have a long night ahead of us."

Felix pushes off the wall, his movements economical and deadly. He walks up to Leon, his eyes unreadable, a faint smile playing on his lips. "Pazienza, Catcher. Always pazienza." He holds up the knife, the tip resting lightly on Leon's chest, just over his heart. "We're going to have a nice, long chat, Leon. Think of it as a business consultation. We're auditing your books. And we're very thorough auditors."

Gabe steps forward, his hands shoved deep into his pockets, his gaze fixed on Leon's face. "Let's start with the easy stuff, Leon. The foundation of your little empire. How many businesses do you have running in Melbourne? Give us the names. The locations. The whole ledger. We want the full scope of your filth."

Leon just laughs, a dry, rattling sound that quickly turns into a cough. "You think I'm going to tell you that? You think I'm going to hand over my empire? You're an animal, Gallo. I'm a businessman."

Aurelio sighs dramatically, pulling a small, clear bag of coarse salt from his satchel. He holds it up to the light, admiring the crystals. "Such a cliché, Leon. The 'businessman' routine. We're not asking. We're telling. And every time you refuse, Felix gets to play. And Felix plays rough."

Felix nods, his eyes never leaving Leon's. He flicks the knife, and a thin crimson line appears just below Leon's ribcage, a precise, shallow cut that barely breaks the skin but promises deep, burning pain. The blood wells up, dark and thick. It's a perfect line, a signature.

"That's just the beginning, Leon," Felix purrs, his voice a low, musical drawl. "We call this the amuse-bouche. Now, the salt."

Aurelio steps up, his face a mask of bored professionalism, and sprinkles a generous pinch of the coarse salt directly into the fresh wound. Leon screams, a high-pitched, desperate sound that bounces off the concrete walls, his body convulsing violently against the chains.

"The names, Leon," Gabe presses, his voice flat, a dangerous calm settling over him. "Start talking. We don't have all night. My wife is expecting me home."

Leon gasps, his body still shaking. "The... the clubs. Three of them. The Serpent's Kiss in Richmond. It's a high-end brothel. The Black Swan in Docklands. That's a private gambling den. And... and The Red Room in St Kilda. That's... that's where the girls are sold. That's all I have left; you have taken over the others..."

"Addresses?" I demand, stepping closer, my shadow engulfing him.

He gives us the addresses, his voice shaking as the words tumble out in a desperate rush. Felix makes another cut, this time a long, shallow slice on his inner arm, just where the soft flesh meets the muscle. It's a deeper cut this time, the blood flowing freely, leaving a path of red down his torso, a bright ugly red. Aurelio follows with the salt. Leon's screams are louder now, more desperate, more broken.

"What else, Leon? Clubs are small fry. What else have you done in the city exactly?" Gabe asks, his voice rising in intensity, the calm starting to fray. "We know you're bigger than this. The money. The drugs. The weapons. The whole network. Don't insult our intelligence."

Leon tries to look defiant, but the pain is winning. "They're... they're just product. I move them. I sell them. It's a business. A necessary one. I'm a distributor! I don't get my hands dirty with the logistics!"

"Lies," I snarl. "You're a coward who hides behind a desk. But you're still responsible. Felix, the first souvenir."

Felix's hand shoots out, grabbing Leon's left pinkie finger. He places the knife blade against the joint. "This is where the business ends, Leon. Tell us about the network, or this finger goes to Felix as a souvenir. He's got a nice little collection started."

Leon screams, begging. "No! Please! I'll tell you! It's a pipeline! From Serbia, through Dubai, into Melbourne! My boss in Serbia handles the logistics! I just handle the distribution! The buyers are all over the city! They're untouchable! They're the ones with the real power!"

"Ok," My voice a cold comfort. "We need the names of your partners."

Leon rattles off a few names, local businessmen, low-level politicians and a few judges. Felix cuts the finger off anyway. The sound is a sickening slice, a wet, sharp noise echoing in the silence after Leon's scream. The finger drops to the floor, twitching like a grotesque, pale slug. Leon's scream is a raw, animal sound of pure agony, a sound that tears at the fabric of the warehouse.

"That was for the delay," Felix explains, wiping the blade on Leon's trousers with a fastidious air.

Leon is a mess of tears, snot and blood. He gives us two addresses, warehouses in the outer suburbs. We already knew about them, but the confirmation is good. Felix cuts the ring finger off. Another snip. Another scream.

"We're running out of fingers, Leon," Aurelio says, his voice suddenly serious, the jaunty tune gone, replaced by a cold, focused intensity. "And you're still holding out. The snuff club, Leon. The one you didn't mention. The one that's not a club. The one where the women don't leave."

Leon's eyes dart wildly. He tries to deny it, his voice cracking. "I don't know what you're talking about! That's not my style! I'm a businessman! I don't deal in… in that kind of filth!"

Felix grabs the next finger, the middle one. He doesn't wait for a refusal. He cuts it off, the knife moving with brutal efficiency. Leon's body spasms violently; the chain rattling like a death knell.

"You're a liar, Leon," I say, my voice flat, the last vestiges of my patience gone. "We know about the one on the outskirts. The one that's more than just a sex club. The one where the women are killed sometimes and pushed under the rug." Angel has been pulling everything apart on his end and found the club in the dark web.

The words hang in the air, heavy and dark. Gabe's face, already pale, turns a sickly shade of green. He takes a step back, his eyes wide with a horror that is visceral and absolute. He's seen a lot of death, but this… this is different. This is a violation of the unspoken rules; a descent into a depravity that even we, the monsters, find repulsive. This is something Angel told us and not Gabe, knowing this would send the man spiralling, his mind would be clouded by Alba and the fact she could have ended up there.

Leon finally breaks. He sobs, a pathetic, broken sound that is barely human. "It's… it's a private thing. For the real high rollers. It's called The Final Curtain. It's a small place, a bunker, really. Out past Dandenong. I only go there to collect the fees. I swear, I don't participate! It's not my business, it's theirs!"

"The address, Leon," Gabe whispers, his voice trembling with a rage that is cold and terrifying, a quiet storm brewing behind his eyes. "Give us the address. Now."

Leon gives the address, a string of numbers and a cross street, his voice a choked, desperate plea for mercy.

Gabe doesn't wait for Felix to finish the interrogation. He pulls a knife from his pocket and walks toward Leon. His movements are slow and deliberate; every step a commitment towards an irreversible act.

"You son of a bitch," Gabe says, his voice barely audible, a broken whisper of disgust. "You piece of absolute filth. You let them kill women, probably fucking dead corpses, and you just turn up to collect the cash, I don't believe you one bit."

Leon sees the look in Gabe's eyes, the pure, unadulterated fury. He starts to scream, a frantic, high-pitched wail of terror; a sound cut short as Gabe's hand flashes out.

Gabe doesn't hesitate. He stabs Leon in the eye. The knife plunges deep, letting off a sickening, wet sound that is louder than any of Leon's screams. Leon's body goes instantly rigid, before slackening; his body left hanging heavily from the chain with his head tilted at an unnatural angle.

Gabe pulls the knife out, the tip covered in blood and a milky, viscous fluid. He stares at it for a long, silent moment, his chest heaving, his breath ragged.

"That was for the women," Gabe says, his voice a broken whisper, his eyes dark and empty. He looks at me, his face a mask of devastating exhaustion.

Felix walks up to Leon's hanging body and gives it a dismissive kick. "Amateur. I was going to take the other three fingers first. And the toes. You always forget the toes."

Aurelio just shakes his head, a grim look on his face.

He walks over to Gabe, gently taking the knife from his hand. "Some things you don't wait for, Felix. Some things you just need to do. Come on, Gabe. Let's get you cleaned up."

I look at my brothers, my crew. We're monsters, all of us. But we're monsters who protect our own. And the women attached to it.

About Cassandra Doon

Cassandra hates writing about herself in the third person, but here we are. With over 33 novels penned and no signs of stopping, she writes across multiple genres. Unable to be pinned down by just one, you'll find Fantasy, Dark Romance, Young Adult, and even a Detective series in the mix.

Having grown up in a small country town and later lived in the city, Cassandra found a perfect spot she likes to call an 'in-between place'—complete with rolling hills and just a stone's throw from the Gold Coast in Queensland Australia.

While she may have had social media in the past, Cassandra has since declared it's not for her. Her website is now the best place to find out what's happening in her world and to see what upcoming books are on the horizon.

a

Also by Cassandra Doon

The 4 Seats Series:

Matteo

Felix

Gabriel

Catcher

Ruhn & Frost

The 4 Seats Extended World:

Aces

Obsessed Shadows

Adrian Romano

The Moretti Brothers (Coming Soon)

Standalone:

The Kings of Willows Peak

Damaged Goods 

Tuesday May

The Devils Cut

The Detectives Mate

Dark Dahlias Rite

A Field of Tulips and Bones

Follow Poppy

To Her

Blood moon

Unit 9

Broken Creek Ranch

Eclipsion (Coming Soon)

The Dead Zone (Coming Soon)

~

Oakland Harbour Series:

Missing

Found

Home

~

The Boys Series

The Boys Of Hastings House

The Boys of Bittersweet College

The Boys of Nightsbane University (Coming Soon)

The Boys of Winchester U (Coming Soon)

~

Second Chances Series:

The Waterfall

Wicked Bonds

Writhe (Coming Soon)

The Restaurant (Coming Soon)

~

Umbravivus Series:

The Lost Kingdom of Umbravivus (Coming Soon)

The Crowned King of Umbravivus (Coming Soon)

The Queen of Umbravivus (Coming Soon)

~

Butcher and the Witch Series:

Poison is always in the Prettiest Bottle

Candles make Great Alibis

Socials with a Slice of Pie

Also By C.L. Doon

The Rain Dang Detective Series:

Still Waters

Moving Waters (coming Soon)

Standalone:

Second Chances at The Riverbend Café

Lavender (Coming Soon)

Also By C. Doon

Standalone:

Ravenwood Manor

Phantom Navis